IS IT FOUR O'CLOCK YET?

by the same author

You, Me and Destiny

September 1997

It was a day on which everything seemed to signal a fresh start. Stephen Daly had arrived in a new town to begin his first day in his first job. It was also the start of a new school year, that momentous day when excitement and trepidation tussle for dominance and for a brief period, almost anything seems possible. As Stephen walked through the gates of Saint Jude's College, even the weather saluted the occasion. After a long unsettled spell, there was unseasonable warmth in the early morning shown brightly from a cloudless sky. But, most importantly, that first day in September represented his deliverance from a constrained and stifled social life. At twenty-two years of age, the young Dubliner was still innocent in the ways of the world, and he was anxious to put that right.

Stephen had lived at home during his college years. As a result, he had missed out on much of the student experience. He was usually tucked up in his bed while his classmates partied endlessly in student haunts or made out in grotty little flats. Yet, he was far from being unsociable by nature. Stephen had the occasional female companion, but he had never been in a serious relationship. It was generally a case of a few drinks, a burger and chips on the way home and just maybe a quick snog at the bus stop before parting company. No girl had yet stolen his heart. Nevertheless, he hoped that there was some special girl, waiting for him, once he had wriggled free of the straitjacket of academia and family ties. With his family over a hundred miles away in Dublin, Stephen considered that he was now free to start enjoying a whole social life. He was looking forward to writing the first glorious chapter in his professional and personal life. Pretty soon, he hoped that he would have money in his pocket, joy in his life and a girl on his arm.

Standing just over six feet tall, he was of a slim, athletic build with recently trimmed dark brown hair. The unkempt look, the hallmark of his student days, had been abandoned, as had the military fatigues and his favoured Dr Martens. Although he had rugged good looks and an agreeable manner, he was charmingly unaware of these appealing qualities. Had he known this, the college's bright reading rooms might well have seen a little less of him and the dim recesses of the college bar a little more.

Seventeen years earlier, his twin brother had been killed in a road accident. Conor's tragic death had left a dark cloud over the Daly household that had proved impossible to shift. Even though his parents had moved house on more than one occasion, they could never distance themselves from that tragic event. The resultant sombre atmosphere in the home was not conducive to youthful exuberance, and Stephen was too conscious of his parents' anguish to play the role of the carefree youth. In recent times, he imagined that even his presence was a constant reminder to them of his identical brother.

Now that he had earned a professional qualification, Stephen saw this as the ideal time to make a fresh start in new surroundings. His parents agreed, believing that it was finally time to lay the ghosts of the past to rest. Life was to be lived, and if Stephen did not start living his life soon, then that awful accident would have claimed the lives of two brothers.

His efforts at securing a teaching position were rewarded when he landed a one-year contract in an all-boys school in Castlehome. This small town may have been little more than a sleepy backwater, a glorified village to Stephen Daly. Still, to its inhabitants, it most definitely ranked as a town and one of some consequence. With a population of some ten thousand people, it was enjoying its share of prosperity. Castlehome was a centre of employment for hundreds of people, boasting a Regional Hospital, three medium-sized hotels, and an assortment of financial institutions. It experienced rush-hour traffic jams and had even a light controlled roundabout.

Although Stephen had initially been employed on a one-year contract, the situation could be reviewed at the end of the school year. However, he hoped that with a year's experience under his belt, he could be in line for a permanent contract. Even the school principal, Simon Lynch, seemed optimistic about Stephen's long-term prospects when paying him a dubious compliment after his successful interview.

'You are a young man of average intelligence, and more importantly, you are well connected'.

Stephen's late uncle, Rev. Malachy Dillon, had served in the religious order, which still managed St. Jude's secondary school for boys. That piece of information helped to unlock the door for him. Stephen had rightly concluded that if the old school tie worked for some people, why not the Roman collar for him?

Simon Lynch was in his second year as lay principal. Like Stephen, he, too, had the right connections. Belonging to a generation that saw most young men move straight from secondary school to the seminary, Simon had even been ordained a priest and served in that role for several years.

After laicisation, Lynch was still preferred to one who had never worn the habit. A safe pair of hands was what the order wanted, with the conventional rather than the radical, being favoured. Simon Lynch could be relied upon for conservatism. He was as likely to have an original thought as a cat is to turn vegan. At least, under his stewardship, the school was unlikely to be at the centre of any scandals. Even though the college had appointed a lay principal, the religious order was still deeply involved in its management. It may have handed over the reins, but it was still operating the stables.

The main building of the college was a grey and forbidding form, dating back to the 1930s. Huddled around that building like a clutch around the mother hen were structures of more recent construction. These less attractive edifices were a response to the school population's explosion during the seventies following the introduction of Free Education. That explosion was now very much history. When Stephen arrived on the staff, the school was in an unenviable position. Numbers were in decline. The college was not the obvious choice for parents of young boys. There was very keen competition for enrolment with another rival boys' school in town.

Stephen entered the main building through what he wrongly supposed to be the main door. As he navigated his way through the dark and unwelcoming interior, he soon located the staffroom. The loud and animated conversation of the assembled teachers had drifted out through the open door onto the echoing corridor. In the sparsely furnished staffroom, the congregated teachers stood around chatting good-humouredly in loose groups. Stephen felt out of place, like a new tenant, who had aimlessly wandered into a residents' association party.

For such a staff facility, there was a curious lack of furniture. There were few chairs except for a random selection of leather armchairs, which appeared to have originated in an old-folks' home. These had been shoved up against the sidewalls. The only other piece of furniture was a long wooden table reminiscent of the one seen in artistic depictions of the Last Supper. This table was laden with large teapots and an assortment of mismatched crockery. Just as Stephen moved to pour a cup of tea, a rather flustered school principal noticed his arrival.

'Did you sign those forms in the office yet?' Lynch asked.

When Stephen answered in the negative, an irritable Lynch led him to the office.

'I have to take assembly in five minutes, but you focus on getting those forms signed, and we will take it from there'.

If the young teacher had been expecting a welcome and some basic induction, he was to be disappointed. So, Stephen accompanied the irritable and agitated Mr Lynch to the front office where he first met Sharon, the school secretary. Unlike her boss, she seemed to be the epitome of friendliness and calm efficiency. She had seen it all before and realised that the new recruit must be wondering what he had let himself in for.

'I know that things might look a bit chaotic now, but they will settle down. We are not a bad lot, really'.

Stephen was somewhat assured.

'Have you met any of your new colleagues yet?'

'No, I just made it to the staffroom and saw groups of them chatting, but Mr Lynch brought me over here to sign some documents'.

Sharon promptly produced the relevant forms for his signature. Stephen duly obliged.

'That's it. You are one of us now'.

Stephen smiled as graciously as he could, considering the anxiety he felt.

'Do you know where your classroom is?' the secretary asked.

'I wasn't told anything at all', Stephen confessed.

Sharon was not at all surprised. She reached to grab a copy of the map of the classrooms with the respective teacher occupants.

'Yea, I have got you here. You are in Room 3 on the second floor over the church.'

That piece of information meant precious little to the new man, and his face reflected his discomfort.

Sharon emerged from behind her desk and pointed to the building opposite.

'Do you see the stain-glass windows on the ground floor?'

Stephen could easily make out the distinctive windows and the entrance door in the centre of the building.

'Just inside that door is a staircase there. Go up two flights of stairs. Your room is the third one in from the landing'.

Sharon suddenly recalled that there had been some issue with the key of that classroom.

'I have no key for that room, but I know that Peter, our caretaker, is mopping up a spillage on that corridor now. So, if you wander up there now, he will be able to open your classroom door for you'.

That sounded like a sensible suggestion.

The caretaker had just finished mopping a soft-drink spillage on the corridor when he observed the new staff member try the handle of a classroom door. He moved towards him, instinctively fumbling through his set of keys for the one, which would allow the young man access to his new work area.

'Not a bad morning! You must be the new teacher Lynch mentioned', he said by way of introduction.

Stephen assured him that he was that new teacher.

'We had to change the lock on this one. I'll open up for you now if you give me one second to get this bucket out of your way. And we will have to cut a copy of it for you.'

With the bucket cleared from the doorway, Stephen thrust out his right hand and introduced himself. The middle-aged man gripped his hand firmly and warmly returned the courtesy.

'I'm Peter Maher. As you can see, I'm a sort of caretaker and general dog's body around here,' he laughed.

Stephen felt obliged to say something complimentary, as the man seemed a rather friendly sort.

'I'm sure the place wouldn't survive long without you', he remarked.

'None of us is indispensable', Peter replied before satisfying his curiosity on the new man's origins.

'What part of the country are you from yourself?

'Dublin', the young man replied.

'Where in Dublin? It is a big place', Peter queried.

'Well, if you know the city, you will know where Castleknock is. That's my home area'.

Peter was familiar with Dublin, having worked there for some years and knew exactly where the place was.

'I know it well, that's not very far from the zoo', he laughed.

'At least you'll feel at home here!'

The older man's levity only served to deepen the anxiety levels of the younger man. Stephen felt a knot forming in his stomach.

'Like the zoo! Are you serious?' Stephen asked with more than a hint of concern on his face.

'Well, I suppose the only difference is that you don't have to get into the cages with the animals in the zoo,' Peter joked.

Stephen was not in the mood for such humour, and it showed.

'Listen, I'm only winding you up, but there is a wild streak to young fellows nowadays. I'm sure that's true for most schools in the country'.

It was difficult to disagree with that.

'There are some wealthy people around Castleknock', the caretaker remarked.

Stephen was well aware that it was viewed as an affluent area, but such generalisations hide much of the truth.

'I suppose, but there are also ordinary people there who are struggling to get by. We moved from Portlaoise some years back, so we are not exactly natives'.

The older man had just been engaging in good-natured banter and hadn't expected to be taken seriously.

'Jaysus! I was only joking about the place. I did a bit of building work in the zoo once. I worked with a construction firm in Dublin for years.

Then my father got sick, so I had to come back home. But anyway, I better have less chat and let you in here.'

In a moment, Stephen's classroom was thrown open to him.

This room would become the arena where he would have to prove himself.

'I'll have to nail a bit of ply-board to cover that hole there', Peter said, pointing with his foot to a damaged panel midway down the door.

'Some thick must have put his boot through it', he said, shaking his head in disgust at such wanton destruction.

'And that was done this morning when they could not have been more than five minutes in the place', he said with disbelief.

The door was thrown open. Stephen thanked the caretaker and entered the room to await his fate.

The young Dubliner felt a further tightening in his stomach as he surveyed the dilapidated room. He could smell the fresh paint and see that an effort had been made to make the space more presentable. However, the room was light years behind what he had been used to. Then again, his schooling had taken place in quite a new building.

He sat in the teacher's chair and pulled open the drawers in the desk. There was nothing there apart from an old duster. Through the vandalised door, he could see onto what was still a deserted corridor. As the clock on the wall ticked past 9.40, he was growing increasingly anxious. In a few moments, thirty energetic and bustling teenage boys would noisily charge down that corridor to his classroom. A cold sweat broke out all over his body. He tried desperately to compose himself.

Peter Maher might just be a humble janitor. Still, this man had a better idea of what went on in Irish schools than all the academics he had listened to in college. Peter saw the reality every day, whereas the academics were disconnected from that reality. During his school days, he had witnessed several teachers fall victim to the classroom ruffian. The fear of suffering that same fate galvanised him. So, having studied the room's layout, he rearranged the seating to allow him access to all areas.

The ringing of the bell was the stimulus, and the response was immediate.

Wave after wave of chattering, boisterous youths streamed into every passageway, wilfully creating bottlenecks and delighted at the prospect of an almighty mosh. Shrill voices of unseen teachers could be heard shouting unheeded warnings and reprimands at the virtual tsunami of uniformed boys. The total number on the corridors was quickly reduced as successive classrooms absorbed their quotas. Now, it was his turn.

The nervous, young teacher sternly watched his new students and steeled himself to play his new role as the authoritative figure. He sternly surveyed his newly acquired students. They similarly studied him. This class was a Third Year class, and Stephen Daly was responsible for their English language and literature education. Once everyone was seated, he launched into his well-rehearsed performance.

'My name is Mr Daly. I will be your English teacher. I should warn you, at the outset, that I have high standards and that I expect the same from you. I adopt a no-nonsense approach. Therefore, the sooner you realise that, the easier it will be for you all'.

These potentially unruly boys sat quietly and listened attentively to him as he desperately hoped that he appeared plausible in his new role.

I intend to be fair but very firm too. Any boy who behaves and does his work will have nothing to fear from me, but I will come down like a ton of bricks on anyone who interrupts learning'.

So far, so good!

Things were going much better than he had expected.

To limit the scope for disorder and allow him further time to compose himself, Stephen prescribed a written assignment to be completed in class.

As he paced imperiously between the now orderly rows, the only sound was that of firm writing on crisp, yielding paper. He felt good. This was where so many weaker spirits would have wilted. As the janitor wisely said, it was simply a case of showing them that he was in charge. The boys had seen him as a man to be taken seriously. He was going to enjoy this. He was simply doing what the textbooks and lecturers described as *Establishing an atmosphere conducive to learning*.

What more could a man be expected to achieve on his first day? Certainly, there was the sound of giggling outside his door, but that was not his responsibility. Then, inexplicably, the classroom erupted in uproarious laughter. Stephen was at a loss as to the cause of this sudden disorder. There was no obvious explanation. He did not have the experience to handle this situation. He roared for silence, but the volume of the riotous laughter drowned his shouts out. He observed their heads turning and looking towards the door, but he could see no explanation there. He suspected that this had been a prearranged plan, but it seemed too spontaneous for that. Stephen felt helpless. His shouts, threats and appeals were all in vain. He was floundering and on the verge of tears. He had not planned for such an eventuality.

Then, suddenly, the cause of the disturbance revealed itself. Some outlaw on the corridor had let down his trousers and was now shamelessly displaying his bare backside through the bashed out panel of the door. Its moon-like orb was neatly framed as it teased the class to convulsions of laughter.

Stephen's reaction was belated and woefully ineffective. He raced to confront the perpetrator. However, it was already too late. He just got a fleeting glance of two uniformed backs and one half-bare

backside exit the corridor and onto the safety of the stairwell. He gave chase but to no avail.
On his return, he could hear the mocking laughter from his classroom. He knew that he should not have left them unsupervised, even for a few moments. That had been a cardinal sin on his part.

The bare-assed scoundrel had escaped. Stephen stood rooted to the spot, with disappointment and frustration competing for supremacy within him. Luckily for him, the school bell signalled the end of class. Otherwise, he would have had difficulty bringing the boys down from that high of excitement. He then watched, from the far end of the corridor, the sight of his class stampede in the opposite direction, eager to relay the story of the new teacher's humiliation to the rest of the students. Stephen trudged dejectedly back to his classroom, kicking its door behind him, bashing out a second panel.

It had been an inauspicious start for the raw recruit. Stephen's immediate priority was attempting to recover respectability in the classroom. He had no idea that a single bare backside could cause him so much bother. He would not live that one down in a hurry. He decided against reporting the incident. Apart from being too embarrassing, it would likely be viewed as a damning episode for him. As it happened, there was, however, no need to report it. The school grapevine was in overdrive. Before lunchtime, the entire school knew the story, with numerous embellishments.

Corrigan, the Maths teacher, was the first to mention it as he arrived to take a class in the room next to Stephen.

'Heard they were making faces at you through the door', he joked.

Stephen's face turned a bright shade of red.

'News travels fast', Stephen replied limply, silently cursing how fate had ruined his debut and turned him into a laughing stock.

'And I thought all the ass holes were in my class', continued Corrigan, laughing heartily at his witticism.

'Good to meet you lad, Jimmy Corrigan is my name', he said, reaching out his hand in friendship towards him.

'Stephen Daly, I'm pleased to meet you'.

Just as Stephen was beginning to dismiss Corrigan as another smart Alec, the older man showed a more fatherly side of his character.

'Stephen lad, don't let it put you off in the slightest. The principal here tolerates that sort of behaviour, so we just have to do our best to keep the bastards in check.'

Jimmy Corrigan was now in full flow on this, his pet subject. He could write a Master's Thesis on the shortcomings of school principals in general and on Simon Lynch in particular.
'It's all about the numbers with them, quantity over quality every time'.

These two men were to become great friends despite the twenty-year age gap between them. Jimmy had honesty and irreverence that the younger man found refreshing.
James Pius Corrigan, known to his friends as Jimmy, had been on the teaching staff in St. Jude's for twenty years. This giant of a man from Cashel, Co. Tipperary stood out in the school as prominently as the iconic rock in his native town.
He should never have been a teacher. His temperament did not suit the job. His one great passion was curiously enough soccer, not hurling as might be expected from a man from the Premier County.
References to soccer peppered his speech. He saw life in terms of being one extended soccer match with very definite winners and losers. In his own terminology, Jimmy was a couple of goals down in the great game of life.
After many years of separation from an American girl, he was now a divorced man. He had met Gloria when she was working as a waitress in a Dublin restaurant. She had been working her way around Britain and Ireland, experiencing the culture and lifestyle. However, she appeared to have sampled a bit too much of Jimmy Corrigan's wares. This Tipperary man fitted the tall, dark, handsome ideal of her youthful dreams.

Corrigan, as he might say himself, kicked off before the whistle. This resulted in Gloria being prematurely cast in the role of an expectant mother. Jimmy had an old fashioned sense of duty, so a wedding was hastily arranged. Tragically, Gloria's baby was not long for this world, dying within a few months of its birth. Their relationship was buried with the baby. Shortly afterwards, Gloria returned to America, while Jimmy never dated another girl afterwards.

Corrigan's professional life was as problematic as his love life. In class, he showed little in the way of patience, and unfortunately, much in the form of impatience. He was not averse to stating what he would like to do to particular students, who might incur his renowned wrath. This practice caused problems for Jimmy and, by extension, for the principal. Parents were threatening everything from litigation to kneecapping. Despite all this, Jimmy seemed incapable of change. 'You have to keep manners on the little fuckers,' he would argue as if his approach was an eminently reasonable one.

As Stephen and Jimmy chatted, their conversation was interrupted by an announcement over the school public address system. The school secretary communicated some changes to the timetable before finishing with a request that Mr Daly report to the principal's office.

'You better go and see what that fool wants this time', said Jimmy irreverently.

As the young man headed towards the principal's office, Jimmy called after him.

'Do you think Lynch is going to organise an identity parade so that you can identify the arse, which appeared in your door?' He asked, laughing at the very thought.
But, for Stephen, this was no laughing matter. He dolefully shook his head before facing in the direction of the office.

An impolite growl from inside was the signal to enter the principal's door. Simon Lynch was an old-world character, uncertain of his place in the modern world, which he did not understand or appreciate. Almost every aspect of his life represented a throwback to a by-gone age.

At school, he continued to wear the black academic gown, long discarded by his contemporaries. His suits were of the three-piece variety, typically Donegal tweed, with no concessions to seasonal factors. Many among his staff doubted whether he even discarded this attire when going to bed.

The most surprising thing about Lynch was that he was married to an attractive, younger woman and had two teenage daughters. If Lynch landed a woman, there was hope for the rest of mankind.

Stephen Daly stood beside the principal's desk, waiting to have his presence acknowledged. On the desk before Mr Lynch sat files containing mostly hand-written notes, as well as the unopened morning post. The principal cleared his throat. Stephen felt his heart missed a beat as anxiety again took hold of him.

'Ah, Stephen, there you are. Take a seat'.

In his heart of hearts, he knew that this summons had to be, in some way, related to the bare backside incident.

Lynch immediately got to the point.

'I heard about the little incident in your classroom', he began.

Stephen could feel his face reddening with embarrassment.

He felt compelled to speak in his defence.

'Well, actually, Mr Lynch, that incident occurred on the corridor outside of my classroom. My classroom door had been kicked in, and a panel was missing.'

As he spoke, Stephen searched Lynch's face for some sign of understanding or at least of compassion. That search had proved fruitless. Lynch just sat there, grey-faced and expressionless. He was like an old judge, who had heard all the excuses and extenuating circumstances and had grown cynical over the years.

'There was messing outside on the corridor. Then this thing appeared. My class broke up laughing at it. But it all happened outside on the corridor, I assure you'.

'I see, but all this business is very bad for the image of the college. It is not the type of story we want circulating.'

Stephen soon realised that he was being blamed for the incident.

'It wasn't even in my classroom.'

Such pedantic distinctions were lost on the long-suffering principal. So, Simon Lynch began his oft-rehearsed speech to new staff members, who had their first exposure to unruly misbehaviour in the college.

'We have a great bunch of boys here, charming lads. I would go so far as to say; they are the finest in the country'.

As he spoke, the principal sat back in his well-worn leather chair.

'Now, of course, I accept that one or two can, at times, be lively or giddy. I see it as a challenge for all of us. We have to make these few bold boys see the error of their ways. God bless them'.

Lynch wondered aloud whether a positive identification had been made of the offending rear end.
Stephen had been tempted to remind his boss that he was new to the school, and one arse looked much the same to him as another. However, being in such a precarious situation, he dared not risk alienating his boss in his first hour on the job.
'I only saw their backs Mr Lynch', answered the young man.
'Yes, their backs', the old man mused, anticipating many insurmountable problems in narrowing down likely culprits.

The principal believed that the current crop of new teachers needed more support than he was inclined to offer. He was not, however, disposed to wasting his valuable time on the matter. In his opinion, student discipline was an issue for individual teachers. There would be no overarching disciplinary approach while he was in charge or no support system for new teachers.
From his perspective, there were more pressing problems, such as the parent threatening to sue the school over Corrigan's verbal onslaught on a student before class had even started.
After what was for Stephen, a moment of self-conscious silence, Lynch spoke again.
'I have good news for you, Stephen; the caretaker is going to fix that door of yours this evening, so leave the door open after class like a good boy.'
Stephen stood up to leave, assuring the principal that he would leave his room unlocked as requested.

'And Stephen, remember that nice and easy does it with the boys. After all, we have to bring them with us. We can't be fighting with them all the time'.

Lynch excused Stephen, reassuring him that his door would always be open to him if he experienced further problems.

Stephen thanked him before taking his leave.

Lynch had very cleverly laid down two significant markers for Stephen. The first was that the college's reputation was paramount. Secondly, a teacher will be held responsible for any misbehaviour on the part of students in his classroom. So, as far as school management was concerned, Stephen Daly could sink or swim. Either way, he was on his own.

For his first days in Castlehome, Stephen lodged in a B & B on the Dublin Road. While the accommodation was certainly up to standard, it was quite limiting for a young man with such romantically ambitious plans. Furthermore, he had not travelled over a hundred miles from Dublin to exchange one mother figure for another.

The college provided the contact details. Mrs Eileen O' Dea was a pillar of respectability in the Castlehome community.
Stephen speculated that Eileen might have been a different sort of pillar had she lived in Biblical times like the unfortunate Lot's wife. She was a curious woman who had an insatiable appetite for news and gossip. She was known as *Forty Questions* because she asked more questions than a quiz show host in a speed round.
Stephen was more than willing to engage in the usual small talk over breakfast. Still, he did not feel like sharing family information. This was a particularly sensitive subject for him.

Eileen was keen to know what his father and mother did for a living and how many siblings he had. Stephen became defensive when pressed for such information. The details of his background, tragic and all as they were, might readily have been relayed to her if she had not been so transparently curious.
Stephen had two younger sisters, Niamh and Lorraine, who were still at school in Dublin. His twin brother, Conor, had been tragically killed in a road accident some seventeen years earlier. At that time, the family lived in Portlaoise. His father currently worked in Administration, in Dublin City Council. His mother worked full-time

in the home. Prior to that, she had been employed as an Air Hostess with *Aer Lingus*.

Stephen had to get out of the B and B. It was doing his head in. But where was he to go? A single flat or an apartment did not appeal to him at all. He felt the need for some company if he were not to go to seed completely.

Sharing a house was the most desirable option.

Pamela Mc Enroe was also new to the teaching staff. She taught French and was substituting for another teacher, who had taken a year out as a volunteer with *Goal*, the Third World Agency. Pamela seemed pleasant and friendly. Stephen could easily imagine being friends with her.

Unlike him, Pamela had her accommodation sorted. She had a local contact, which resulted in her sharing a house with young nurses on a newly-built housing estate.

Tom Clarke, another homeless colleague, was also keen to share a house. On the first day of term, he had approached Stephen on the subject. They had agreed to share as soon as suitable accommodation presented itself.

The two of them maintained a close eye on the local paper. However, they were not optimistic about a quick fix to their accommodation problems, as the rental accommodation sector in Castlehome was not particularly strong.

Tom and Stephen were eventually rewarded for their patience. A house in a newly built estate off the Galway road became available for rent. Pamela was living in the same estate. The boys now shared with Frank

Smith and Seamus Dunne, who worked in the local *Bank of Ireland* branch. Judging by appearances, the two lads seemed to be suitably house trained and friendly. Moreover, these two were exceptionally sharp dressers, wearing smart suits to work each day. By contrast, the teachers looked decidedly shabby in their ill-fitting sweaters and creased pants.

The bank officials were seldom at home after work. Apart from normal socialising, their employers had encouraged them to become involved in community and sporting organisations. Tom and Stephen were less community aware. Joining anything that held out the prospect of introductions to the young women of Castlehome and surrounding areas was more their concern. They were not a bit concerned about promotion. They were as likely to end up supermodels as they were to become school principals.

Stephen's mother rang her son on several occasions each week. She was fascinated to hear how things were going for him. Stephen was always short on detail. He never sent her away with a broken heart, no matter how bad things were at school. She had enough heartbreak in her life already without hearing how badly he was doing in his new job.

He always assured her that the teaching was going well and that he was making friends. His mother wanted her son to be happy more than anything else. Since his twin brother had been killed, her priorities had changed. She wanted her remaining son to live his own life as his own man and not as the surviving twin. Conor, his brother, had been denied that opportunity.

His young sisters were hugely proud of their big brother, who was now a fully-fledged teacher. They naively presumed that things were going well for him, jokingly asking about possible introductions to his more handsome senior students. They also asked about how it felt to be in charge of a classroom, which he was unqualified to answer. Stephen listened to all of their enquiries and gave the answers they wanted to hear. He could not let them in on the awful truth of how he was in an ongoing battle for survival, enduring both ridicule and humiliation. Stephen was going to keep that to himself.

Over the weeks, Stephen had met quite a few people, mainly through contacts with other teachers. He quite fancied one of these girls, who shared with his colleague Pamela. Sinead O'Shea was a nurse in the Regional Hospital. Stephen was immediately attracted to this tall brunette with dark eyes and a fantastic smile.

It was a classic case of love at first sight. He fully intended to ask her out on a date but decided to leave it until he first tested the water. He didn't wish to be impulsive and risk looking foolish for making the wrong call. After all, the girl might already be in a relationship with a man or a woman, for that matter. A hasty or clumsy move on his part could well impair his future chances. Stephen would bide his time and as Corrigan would say: 'See how the ball hops'.

At night Stephen and Tom Clarke typically frequented the local pub, *Taylor's*. Although lacking in modernity and comfort, it would be difficult to beat for atmosphere. A traditional style pub run by Shay Taylor and his family had a welcome for all. Musicians were particularly encouraged, and many great sessions took place there.

With bare flagstones on the floor and furniture that presented the stressed look before that particular look ever became popular, it nevertheless carried on a roaring trade. It was particularly popular with undemanding young, fun-loving people. Many romantic relationships had their beginnings there and their endings, also, if the truth were told.

As in any Irish town, the bars often served as the centre of community life. People of all ages and background mingled there. Young people could socialise there and quite possibly meet the love of their lives there. Stephen was interested in meeting people, but the pub was already taking on another role for him. It was fast becoming a place where he could ease the pain and frustration of his working day. He soon discovered that, in the short term, at least, the more he drank, the less pain he felt.

In Taylor's, Stephen first became aware of his colleague and housemate Tom Clarke's musical talent. Up to now, at least, they had relatively little contact with each other, despite working in the same school and sleeping under the same roof. In the college, Tom's classroom was across the schoolyard, in a different building.

In the pub, Tom was a revelation. He was a truly versatile performer. According to Shay Taylor, Tom was so musical he could fart The National Anthem in tune. That was high praise indeed. For a man of twenty-three, Tom could quite easily be mistaken for a senior student. Looking younger than one's years is not usually a problem, but Tom occasionally had trouble getting served in some pubs. It was particularly annoying, as Tom enjoyed more than the occasional pint of beer. Furthermore, how he dressed did little to dispel the teenage look. The man appeared to live on bottles of *Fanta Orange* and *Mars* bars. Tom generally sported a Manchester United top out of school, complete with a baseball cap, peak to the rear, of course. Like the rest of the staff, his dress became decidedly more casual as the weeks elapsed. It was as if the teachers started the new school year with great intentions regarding professional appearance but gradually reverted to the scruffy look.

Tom, like Stephen, had his share of problems in the classroom. On one occasion, he was at the wrong end of a vicious left hook from a senior student, who didn't seem to realise that the fresh-faced young man with the bottle of orange was a teacher. Tom did not like to be reminded of that. It did his street credibility no good at all.

As September wore on, the bell to mark the end of the school day had become more and more the knell of deliverance for both young teachers. It marked a release from their separate hells to a world of ease and relaxation outside the wrought iron gates of St. Jude's. For both, the prospect of life after four o'clock made the school day that little bit more bearable. But how long could that last?

On a cold and blustery October morning, Stephen met Jimmy Corrigan just outside the school gates.

'Ah, Stephen, you look like the Wreck of the Hesperus. A hard night was it?'

The black rims under his eyes testified to his extended presence in the smoke-filled pit, which was Taylor's. With just a few hours of sleep, Stephen felt particularly fragile.

'Thanks for the compliment, Jimmy. It was just the boost I needed', replied Stephen, as he stroked the itchy stubble on his unwashed face.

'Yea, we had a few drinks and a bit of craic in town,' Stephen yawned as he headed for the staff room and the now obligatory pre-class cup of strong coffee.

'Ah, hold your horses for a minute', pleaded Corrigan.

'I can't start the day without a fag. Some of the women would skin you if you lit up inside. They would banish smokers to the ball alleys if they could'.

Corrigan clearly had issues with many of the women on the staff. Even though it was just three years to The Millennium, his attitudes were firmly rooted in old prejudices.

'Take one', he offered, pushing the packet of cigarettes towards Stephen.

'No, thanks! I gave them up after the exams'.

'Wise fucking man! I wish I could give the fucking things up. Still, I can't see me doing that while I'm serving my sentence in this dungeon, he reckoned.

The two men became aware of the principal approaching them. Lynch's black academic gown was gently blowing in the stiff morning breeze. Corrigan nudged Stephen.

'Will you look at the get-up of him, wandering around, like a demented crow.

Is it a bird? Is it a plane? No, it's S-U-P-E-R S-I-M-O-N.'

Stephen smiled at this depiction of their sombre principal, briefly imagining Lynch, like Clarke Kent, wearing his underpants outside of his trousers. Simon Lynch cut a rather risible figure as he meandered his way through hordes of late-coming students, who threatened to upend him at a given moment. It was more a case of Radar Lynch.

An incongruous item of Lynch's attire was a red silk tie firmly secured by a tiepin, with its end underneath the waistband of his trousers.

'Anchored to the bollocks!' Corrigan declared.

'He must have heard a warning about high wind in the weather forecast.

Simon Lynch, never suspecting that he might be the butt of this particular joke, excused his interruption and addressed Stephen.

'I understand that you have Second Year English class to start your day, Stephen', he stated in an untypically pleasant manner.

He must be looking for something, Stephen guessed.

Beware when the boss is nice to you!

'I think so', Stephen replied wondering what particular favour was being sought.

The principal outlined the situation.

'I'm placing a new boy in your class from today', Lynch informed him. 'His name is Martin Greene. The family is new to town. They are fine, professional people. Martin is a boy who is not as robust as the others. Neither would he be as savvy as his peers, or so I am told'.

'More fucking trouble', muttered Corrigan under his breath but still audible to his younger colleague. Thankfully, the principal's hearing was not as sharp as it had once been.

'Martin's parents have been advised that he would be more challenged in your normal mainstream school, rather than in the special school he attended down in Limerick,'

'They think here is normal, do they?' Corrigan interjected.

Lynch treated this remark with silent contempt. He was not to be put off his line of thought.

He informed Stephen that the young boy would only attend class in four subjects for a specific trial period. He would review the situation after a few weeks. Even though it didn't directly concern him, Corrigan wanted more information on this lad's specific learning difficulties. He rightly anticipated that he might well be joining one of his classes in the not distant future. On this point, Lynch was suspiciously vague.

'He is fifteen years old with a mind of a ten-year-old, he said,

To sweeten the pill, he made it clear that academic expectations would not be very high.

'But nobody expects you to get top results or anything like that. Essentially, all you have is an extra body in your classroom'.

Lynch made it sound as if the young boy was like something a mortician might casually deposit in the school until it was time to collect him.
Stephen knew that he had little choice but to agree to allow the new boy into his class. He felt sure that Martin Greene had been instructed to join his class. He was just the hired help, after all.
After Lynch departed, Corrigan advised Stephen against being too cooperative in such instances.
'That Lynch is a cute bastard and is not out for your good or for that young lad's good either. He's up to something. I don't want to worry you unnecessarily, but that Greene lad could well turn your classroom into a circus. The smart boys will likely set him up to cause as much confusion and trouble as possible. They'll make a bloody eejit out of him'.
Corrigan had given young Stephen food for thought.
'Yea, but the poor devil is entitled to education the same as the others. I would like to help the lad as much as I can, but I'm not exactly the best fit for him now, am I?'
'Lynch isn't concerned with the lad's welfare. To him, he's just a problem that he's passing on to you, who has no training at all in that area. Anyway, Stephen, keep a good eye on him. If he strays offside, you can look to offload him.'
'I could send him over to your class, Jimmy?'
'Like hell, you will'.

That particular Second-Year class had been one of the least troublesome for him. The boys there were generally well behaved. He hoped that the new boy would not upset the delicate balance.
Arriving in the corridor, he saw that his class was there before him. There were the usual jostling and horseplay; standard behaviour for boys of this age, but nothing untoward was noted. They were quieter than usual, suspiciously quiet in fact. This usually meant that they were up to no good.
It transpired that somebody had stuffed his door lock with chewing gum.
After painstakingly using a compass to dislodge the offending matter from the lock, he eventually gained access. There followed the inevitable rush for the back row.
'Get out of my fucking seat, Kelly or I'll bust you.'
Choosing to ignore such threatening remarks, he scanned the room for the new face. There was no sign of young Greene.
After bickering over elbows onto their desks and rooting through assorted school bags, the class eventually produced exercise copies.

A remarkable fact was that the less interested students tended to carry just one exercise copy for all the day's classes. This versatile jotter was kept tightly rolled and conveniently stuck up the sleeves of their military-style jackets. The uninterested had dispensed with the notion of having a copybook at all. The noise gradually subsided to a low volume hum. It was certainly not total silence, but for Stephen, it was an acceptable level of noise. It was undoubtedly as good as Stephen was going to get. His prepared lesson today was on letter-writing skills. Stephen decided that they would start with the formal letter.

On the blackboard, he drew a template for such a letter. Each student had a blank sheet of paper on his desk to simulate actual letter writing.As Stephen became absorbed in his work, there was a loud knock at the door.

Opening the door, Stephen caught his first glimpse of Martin Greene.

'Are you Mr Daly?' the new arrival enquired breathlessly yet respectfully.

'Yes, I am. You must be Martin. Mr Lynch told me to expect you. Come on in and take a seat'

He was keen to make the unfortunate lad feel at home.

The strategy seemed to work as the young lad visibly relaxed.

'I got lost, Sir. This is a very big place'.

Martin glanced around at his new classmates and seemed alarmed and mystified, in almost equal measure.

Stephen explained what they had been doing and directed him to the blank sheet of paper on his desk.

'Martin, if you don't understand something, put up your hand, and I will explain it to you'.

After much rooting and rustling of paper, he managed to produce a copybook from his school bag, shortly followed by a pencil.

Stephen continued with the class.

'Right then, boys, we will examine the structure of the formal letter. How you layout this type of letter is of great importance.'

The new boy's hand shot up instantly.

'Yes, Martin', said Stephen, silently cursing the interruption yet anxious to make the newcomer feel welcome.
'Sir, when Mammy is writing a letter, she lays it out on the kitchen table, so it won't get creased'.

The class barely suppressed their impulsive laughter.
'Right, I see, Martin. It is important to keep it neat and tidy. However, by layout, I don't mean the surface on which it is placed. I mean the different parts of the letter'.
Stephen strongly suspected that the distinction was lost on poor Martin.
Unperturbed, he continued with the lesson.
'After writing your address and the date, you write the name of the person to whom you are writing. You write that person's name over on this side of the page'. He said, using a pointer to indicate the left-hand side of the page.

One of the more interested boys asked whether that was their full name or just his first name. Stephen explained that one used both the first name and surname of the recipient.
Martin's hand shot up again. Stephen, with more than a little apprehension, invited the animated Martin to speak.
'Sir, what if you are not writing to another teacher. I mean, what if the person has no Sir name?'
This time the boys looked at each other before the penny began to drop. Martin had never heard the word in any different context. The room erupted with convulsions of laughter. The previously well-mannered boys were now wildly strumming their desks in a variant

form of applause. Those who had not heard clearly had the exchange recounted to them. Stephen quickly realised that he could not help little Martin as he could barely look after himself. A hapless Stephen called for order, determined that future contributions from one Martin Greene would be kept to the absolute minimum.

Martin continued to raise his hand for a succession of questions. As diplomatically as he could, Stephen explained that there were, after all, other students in the class. This was not going to become a one-man show.

While stressing the importance of a proper conclusion to a business or formal letter, Stephen asked for a range of appropriate concluding sentences.

There were several good suggestions.

'How might we wrap up the letter?'

Martin was still waving his arm frantically while shouting 'Teacher'.

Stephen finally relented, allowing Martin to offer his suggestion.

'Please, Sir! My mother does it like this. Martin stood up and, holding the sheet with both hands, folded it in half and then folded it again. There was nothing more to be said. For homework, a formal letter was prescribed. The students were allowed to use the remaining few moments of class to get their letters started. Even though it was frowned upon, Stephen decided to commit the cardinal error of leaving a class unsupervised as he sought the sanctuary of the staffroom. He felt that under the circumstances, it was a risk worth taking.

Strong coffee was called for after the Martin Greene episode. Stephen burst unceremoniously into the staffroom, provoking the disapproving looks of some of his more conscientious colleagues. They had been labouring away on bundles of student assignments. Their red pens had been making solid progress against the imposing piles of copybooks until Stephen's noisy and premature arrival had interrupted their rhythm.

The young man was blissfully unaware of his impact as he stood waiting for the kettle to boil. In a moment, Pamela came into the room with an indulgent grin from ear to ear. Pamela fancied Stephen. She saw the young Dubliner as a prospective boyfriend, and she was determined to bring that about. It was unfortunate that the object of her desire did not reciprocate her romantic feelings.

'You look like a girl who has good news to tell', remarked Stephen.

'Do you fancy a cuppa?'

'Yea, go on, Stephen, I could murder a cup'.

As Stephen made the coffee, Pamela told him that she had just got an unexpected free class. The Guidance Counsellor had taken her class to administer some aptitude tests to them.

'You never know your luck. It might be your turn tomorrow.'

'A 3 piece jigsaw would challenge my lot, but they are not the worst behaved, to be fair to them'. Pamela expressed the opinion that it's tougher being a female teacher in a boy's school.

He had been so engrossed in his difficulties that he had never actually considered others.

'They have only the one thing on their minds. At the end of the last French class, I told them that I would soon be doing some oral work. Well, the sounds that they came out with! I will never make that mistake again'.

She even blushed as she recalled the incident.

'Minds like sewers', Stephen agreed, realising how entirely predictable that response had been.

The kettle clicked off on boiling. Stephen made two cups of coffee and handed the fuller one to Pamela.

She thanked him, added some milk and sugar before taking a sip.

'You make a nice cup of coffee, Stephen.

Stephen smiled a curious smile.

'It's not unduly complicated. I just poured the boiling water in on top of it'.

Pamela smiled coyly.

Stephen confessed that making coffee was about the extent of his culinary skills.

'I'm a disaster at cooking. Ask Tom; he'll tell you that the day I cook is the day he heads to the chipper for a takeaway.'

'Do you know what?' Pam chanced, sensing an advantageous opening. 'You should come over to us this evening for your dinner. It's my turn to cook. There will only be the three of us there. One of the girls is on night duty. Bring Tom as well, if you like', she added unconvincingly.

It had been an unexpected invitation. Stephen was glad that he had prematurely abandoned his Second-Year class and the subject of formal letters. He had a more urgent matter on his mind as he wondered whether Sinead might be dining with them also. Under the circumstances, he decided not to pose the position. He also knew that Tom was going to a twenty first-birthday party that evening so she could count him out.

'Do the girls do much in the way of night duty? Stephen was fishing, hoping for some little nugget of information on Sinead's plans for the evening.

'A fair bit, Sarah is on all this week. I think Sinead is on at the end of the month'.

Inwardly, Stephen was punching the air with delight. Maybe the gods were aligning events in his favour.

His delight was barely concealed as he attempted to respond in a matter of fact tone.

'That's great. I might well take you up on that. Tom is at a twenty-first birthday party tonight, but I'll drop over at whatever time suits'.

'We'll aim for seven.'

'That's lovely', said Stephen.

Tonight could well be the start of something interesting if he played his cards right.

After yet another day of struggling to survive in the classroom, Stephen set about sprucing himself up for the dinner invitation. Even though Pamela Mc Enroe had invited him, his mind was entirely focused on making a good impression on Sinead O'Shea. They had already briefly met, but that was only for a few fleeting moments in a crowded pub. This would be a different situation altogether. It would be his first real opportunity to create the desired impression. He had to seize the day if he wanted to make the right impression on her.

He was at a loss as to precisely what image he should project and was in danger of over-thinking the whole issue. He hadn't a clue about Sinead's taste in men, apart from Pamela mentioning that Sinead didn't like brash or arrogant people.

'She likes to cut men down to size'.

It was not what he needed to hear.

This girl was going to be hard work.

When he was worried or anxious to impress, he tended to talk too much. Some would claim that he talked too much anyway. Often he would hear himself utter the most stupid comments and then blush with embarrassment, powerless to control his unbridled tongue. The secret of success, he once read, was to relax, to think before speaking and most importantly, to banish negative thoughts from one's mind.

A hot shower was the first item on the agenda. When Stephen emerged after showering, he had scrubbed himself better than any exfoliation treatment would have done.

Towelling himself dry, he caught a glimpse of his reflection in the bedroom mirror. Turning to view himself from different angles, he was

reasonably pleased with what he saw. With any bit of luck, Sinead might well enjoy the same view before very long.
Shaving could be a tricky operation, so he had to be careful. He certainly didn't want to turn up for dinner with pieces of tissue paper stuck onto his bloodied face like flakes of dandruff on a giant raspberry.
A new blade would give the closest shave, but there would be a danger of drawing blood. On the other hand, a used razor blade was less likely to cut, but then might it provide a smooth shave? These were important decisions, which might turn out to be of critical importance.
Stephen opted for a used razor blade, one he had been using for the previous few days. After several minutes of close attention, he studied himself in the mirror. There was still some stubborn stubble remaining. He opted to apply some more shaving foam and repeat the process. Pity his mother's hair removal cream was not to hand. Maybe he should ask his senior colleague, Miss Hayes if he could borrow hers. On second thoughts, she probably did not use the stuff. He noticed a slight suggestion of a moustache on her upper lip, very fetching in a sergeant-major sort of way.

He applied his spice-scented deodorant liberally over his body, especially in areas where nervousness might make him perspire heavily. Then, to reassure himself that he had used a sufficient amount, he stuck his nose under his armpits. A splash of *Jazz* aftershave then followed for good measure.
Now, what was he going to wear?

He tried on his new denim shirt with his clean, navy jeans, but he considered that the look was too dark.

What about the dark brown leather jacket? No, he didn't think so.

After many fittings and re-fittings, he eventually settled on his denim jacket and jeans, with the dominant blue colour, relieved by a white polo shirt. This garment had been a present from Mum. With his tall build, he cut quite a formidable dash. He gave his hair a good brushing and looked at the reveal in the mirror. It was the best he could manage without resorting to cosmetic surgery.

It was still only six o'clock, but it felt later. In the kitchen, the two bank lads were preparing their evening meal.

'Jaysus, the smell of you', Seamus shouted, curling his nose and fanning the air with his hand.

'Where are you going? It must be a hot date', he said, holding his nose away from Stephen.

'She'll need a bloody gas mask if she wants to get close'.

The boys laughed as Stephen wondered whether, in his anxiety to impress, he had overdone things. Satisfied that the boys were exaggerating the fragrance's strength, he filled them in about the invitation to dine with the girls.

Frank, while turning the lamb chops, looked up.

'Pamela must be into you, big-time', he teased.

'Be careful. An innocent young fellow like you might get gobbled up'.

'If I need you, Frank, I'll let you know'.

'What time is the meal at?' asked Seamus.

'Seven o'clock!'

'You have an hour to wait so.'

Stephen nervously re-hashed his old reliable joke.

'It won't take me long to wait an hour'.

Stephen was unsure as to what he should take to the dinner.

'Do you think I should bring something? You never know what women expect.'

'Better take precautions', Frank advised.

'I'll check if I have any condoms left from the holidays'.

'Knowing your luck with women, they are all still there.' Stephen retorted.

'I was thinking more in the line of a bottle of wine or a box of chocolates?'

Seamus thought that maybe a box of *After Eights* might be acceptable.

'I mean you often see it on the TV'.

'But only in ads for the product', interrupted Stephen

'True, but at the same time, it's a classy type of gift. It's not too expensive, and it generally goes down well.'

Frank remembered seeing a piece on a breakfast show on British television.

'They said that instead of bringing something on the night of the do, the trend is to have flowers sent to the lady on the following day. No self-respecting man brings them anymore, it claimed.'

That raised a few eyebrows among the boys.

'You bring nothing with you. However, the next day you ring a florist and have them send a few flowers and a thank you note,' Frank informed them.

'You're not just a pretty face, Frank', acknowledged Stephen.

His mind was made up.

'That's what I'll do. I'll bring nothing.'

At seven o'clock, Stephen rang the doorbell at Number 22, "The Manor".

A beaming Pamela answered the door and greeted him with a friendly peck on the cheek. She seemed genuinely pleased to see him.

'You're right on time, Stephen,' she said, happily showing him into the living room.

Out of her normal school attire, Pamela looked quite different. She usually wore her dark hair drawn back and tied back in a ponytail. Tonight, it fell gently around her face; its silky sheen, repaying the investment in time and attention. Stephen complimented Pamela on her appearance. She looked radiant and glamorous in a soft and flowing peach-coloured dress. Despite his complimentary remark, she was not the reason for Stephen's presence there.

As for Sinead, she was nowhere to be seen. He hoped that she would make an appearance.

Pamela excused herself for a moment while she tended to something she was cooking. He, therefore, had a moment alone to take in his surroundings. The house he shared with the boys was very similar in design to the girls' house, but the similarity ended there. The boys' place was devoid of those little extra touches that make a house a home. Where he lived was more of a billet than a home.

The girls had turned their house into a veritable palace. There were fancy little ornaments on the mantelpiece, beautifully scented candles burning fragrantly with even some family snapshots on the television. What a change from a sink full of dishes and mug rings on the kitchen table! There was no smell of potpourri on entering the boys' house. It was more likely to be the smell of sour milk competing with that of sweaty socks.

Pamela returned and directed Stephen to the table, which had already been set for the occasion. The sound of Van Morrison singing *Days like This* provided the background sound.

There was nothing wrong with Pamela's memory, reflected Stephen, as he recalled telling her of his liking for Van the Man.

The dining area was dimly lit, and the mood was romantic. All that was missing was the gipsy violinist.

Unfortunately, there was still no sign of Sinead. He had noted that there were three places set. He was not left in suspense for long as Pamela informed him that they would start as soon as Sinead finished her phone call.

In a moment, Sinead joined them. Stephen felt his heart miss a beat as the object of his desire bounded unselfconsciously into his presence. Unlike Pamela, Sinead O'Shea had opted to present what Stephen imagined to be the casually chic appearance. Either that or she couldn't be bothered making any effort at all. She looked comfortable with herself and at ease with the world in her tight-fitting top and faded jeans. Stephen could hardly keep his eyes off her. She sat opposite, with Pamela, commandeering the chair alongside him.

Sinead gave the young man a once over with her well-practised eye.

'How was your day, Stephen?'

Not too bad, I suppose. I am fighting the good fight'.

'Come on, tuck in and enjoy the melon starter', invited Pamela.

Sinead did not seem to have entered into the spirit of the occasion. She was more interested in venting her frustration at the ongoing road works in the area,

'The traffic was mental this evening. It's so frustrating. I would have been faster walking.'

Stephen sympathised with her plight and mentioned that this was one of the few downsides to owning a car.

'You don't have a car Stephen, do you?'

Taking this to be an indication of some interest, Stephen responded earnestly.

'Not yet, but I'm still keeping an eye out for one'.

Pamela seemed disappointed that he had not mentioned this to her. She had portrayed herself as a confidante to the young Dubliner.

'I take a look around the garages in Dublin whenever I get home. I like a bit of power. You can't beat the old turbocharged two-litre.'

Stephen was eager to impress. However, he was wasting his time. Sinead looked up from the table, her face contorted in an expression that was a mixture of disdain and arrogance.

'Men can be such show-offs.'

Pamela immediately came to her friend's defence.

She claimed that she always envisaged the man of her dreams driving a fancy car.

Sinead felt that the dinner guest was yet another man who needed to be brought down a further peg or two.

'I think men who want powerful cars are attempting to compensate for their inadequacies in other areas'.

Her housemate had also set herself up for a barbed comment.
'And I think women, who are attracted to such men, are nothing short of pathetic.'
Stephen was disappointed that Sinead was adopting such an antagonistic stance. He felt that there would be an interesting exchange between the two women once he departed the scene. Sinead was deliberately trying to embarrass her housemate. It was clear that there was no love lost between them.
As for the barbed comments that Sinead directed his way, he was not at all deterred. The good news was that he wasn't being ignored. He knew that he had an uphill struggle ahead of him if he wished to win the opinionated lady. At least he was eliciting some response. For a perceptible moment, there was an embarrassing silence. Finally, Stephen interjected with an ingratiating comment that he hoped might rescue the situation.
'Of course, I also like the *Ford Fiesta.* I would not mind driving one of those either'.
Sinead looked at him, unable to tell if he was having a joke at her expense. For the moment, she held her fire on that front.
Pamela had cooked chicken in a white wine sauce for the main course. It was not just beautifully presented but was very pleasing to the palate. Thanks to the meal and an amazingly generous supply of wine, a more relaxed atmosphere emerged. Pamela produced a packet of *After Eights* to round off the meal. He was glad that he had decided against bringing a box of the same. Van Morrison continued to do the

necessaries, while extended silences were no longer a cause of anxiety for anyone.

Over the space of an hour or so, the discourse at the table became more congenial. Perhaps this was attributed to the soothing effects of the wine or indeed to Sinead's antagonism lessening. A cup of coffee after a meal was one occasion when Stephen missed being a smoker. There are few greater pleasures than to sit cigarette in hand, sipping on a cup of aromatic fresh brewed coffee.

Pamela rose to draw the plum-red drapes as Sinead started to clear the table. Stephen offered to start on the wash-up. Pamela wouldn't hear of it. Wishing to treat his gracious hostesses, he suggested that they adjourn to Taylor's.

Pamela, conscious of being in more formal attire, dismissed this suggestion.

'What! Dressed like this? Are you mad?'

'I think you look great.'

He would have liked to follow the fine wines with a pint of lager.

'Do you? That's nice, but I'd feel totally out of place in this get-up.'

Pamela exercised her veto, so they stayed put. She suggested that she nip down to the video shop to see what was on offer there. As the only gentleman present, Stephen felt an obligation to offer to make the trip Ideally, he wished that Pamela might leave the room and leave him alone with Sinead.

The girls did not trust a man to choose a good video. It was Sinead who jumped up, grabbed her handbag and left the house.

'I could do with some fresh air anyway. Wine makes me very sleepy', she confessed.
Stephen filed away that nugget of information.
When Sinead returned, she placed the video in the VCR.
He had been hoping for a new release, but Sinead had opted for *Fatal Attraction*. He wondered at the thought process behind that choice.
Sinead and Pamela exchanged curious glances but no words passed between them.
As he had seen it before, he found it difficult to concentrate on the action. As with Sinead, the wine was beginning to make him a bit sleepy also. Between the heat of the room and the warm glow induced by the meal, Stephen did not notice himself gently lapsing into the soft and welcoming arms of sleep.

When he awoke, he was mortified. The film credits were already rolling, and the girls were in kinks of laughter at his loud snoring. Sinead, in her best sarcastic tone, expressed regret for keeping him up past his bedtime. Pamela revealed that Sinead had also nodded off for some time during the showing.
'For a good half hour, I was watching it on my own', she complained.
It was certainly time for him to go home. He could advance his case no further on this occasion. He thanked his hostess and took his leave.
Walking through the estate, he couldn't help laughing to himself.
'At least I can honestly tell the lads that I slept with Sinead'.
There was something that he had to remember. He could not quite recall what it was. Suddenly it came to him in a flash.
'Yea, that's right. I must remember to send flowers tomorrow.'

Autumn leaves were abandoning their wind-assailed boughs as the teaching staff converged on St. Jude's. The dry russet remains of the dead leaves were being shepherded out beyond the schoolyard by the first harsh wind of the season. They were soon to become nothing more than a memory of times past, in much the same manner as each year's output of students fades into the blurred picture that is yesteryear.

A chilling air of desolation hung over the place.

The students had been given a free day, but unfortunately, the teachers were not so lucky. A staff meeting meant that teachers presented themselves in the staff room for a ten o'clock start. This free day was, ostensibly, the day promised to the student body to celebrate the wonderful Junior Certificate results.

Of course, these results were the usual mixture of the good, the bad and the downright awful. Still, from a public relations point of view, a free day sent out the right message. For public consumption, the word was that those had been the best results since 1983. Of course, there was no factual basis for such an assertion. It was a case of whatever random year the principal chose to pluck out of thin air.

For the meeting, the chairs in the staff room had been neatly arranged in rows of ten. The front row faced the green covered table, where the principal sat as chairman, together with the recording secretary. Vice Principal Mr Raymond Shaw usually took on the role of Recording Secretary.

Back in August, Stephen would have looked forward to being present at a staff meeting. As a student, he had often wondered what transpired at such meetings. Now, the novelty was over. He realised that they were just another wasted few hours.

The back rows of chairs were always the first to fill. The neat and orderly arrangement of furniture was quickly upset, as one teacher after another grabbed a chair before retreating with it to the backbenches. It was generally considered a bad move to place oneself in the principal's line of vision. There would inevitably be requests for volunteers for every sort of activity. It was more difficult to brazen it out eyeball to eyeball.

Stephen did not fully appreciate how precarious his position was. The smart move for him would be to volunteer for as much extra-curricular work as he could manage. Principals expected young teachers to be hardworking and enthusiastic. If a principal did not see a young teacher trying to impress in his first year, it was unlikely that he would ever strive to impress. There was also the consideration that the greater distance one was from the top table, the greater opportunity one had to engage one's mind on other matters.

The same teachers did much the same things during these regular meetings. Most teachers fixed their gaze on the top table and allowed their minds to go wherever they wished. Several corrected exercise copies, while a few tackled the Irish Times' cryptic crossword. One cosmopolitan staff member liked to peruse the pages of *The Manchester Guardian*.

Jaded night owls like Stephen and Tom sought a location, offering sufficient screening, to have a little snooze.

After the opening prayer, the meeting began with Raymond Shaw reading the minutes of the previous session. It could well have been the minutes of any staff meeting over the last ten years. The same issues were being constantly debated. As Shaw started to read from his typed page, there was a low-level hum of conversation from the assembled tutors.

Stephen Daly studied the vice principal as he read the details of last month's arguments on discipline.

Shaw was within a few years of retirement. He had been in his current role since the early nineteen seventies. He gained his position not because of any particular merit on his part, but his seniority among the lay staff. Having said that, the staff had no problem with him. Quite the contrary; he was, as the saying goes, both a gentleman and a scholar. In his teaching days, he had been a Latin master and was a most capable classroom teacher.

Shaw projected a very pleasant image and had what might be described as a lived-in face. Sportive lines of wrinkles ran merrily alongside his craggy features before disappearing into the gulf that was his pleasant smile. If the teachers viewed him positively, this was nothing to his popularity with the students. He was the avuncular figure, unfailingly civil and courteous. When he needed to reprimand them, he found it very difficult to be severe. Being attacked by Shaw was not something to unduly concern a wayward student.

Mr Shaw had no direct experience of the deterioration in student behaviour, as he was now totally office-bound. Certainly, he had to be timetabled for some few hours of teaching per week.

However, as he was the one who drew up the timetable, he generally took one of the highly motivated classes. Shaw was certainly lucky to have escaped the rigours of classroom life. At his age, it would not have been a pleasant prospect. The increased salary, which accompanied his elevation, had been a welcome bonus for a man with three children at university.

When the minutes were read and adopted, the main business of the meeting commenced.

As with all other establishments, St. Jude's had its own internal politics. Many individuals had their own agendas. Some teachers had their pet subjects, which were frequently aired on such occasions. Management also needed to relay certain messages to the staff as a whole.

Today, Lynch had one specific complaint to make. He considered that certain teachers were falling down in some respects.

He informed them that a worrying looseness in relation to punctuality had developed. Such tardiness was proving detrimental to school discipline.

Corrigan, sensing that this was a sideswipe at him, saw red and forcefully interjected,

'Do you mean to tell me that teachers going to class two or three minutes earlier would prevent student misbehaviour? We come back here year after year, with the same hole in our arse, debating the same issues, yet nothing is ever done about these problems. We are either serious about imposing sanctions for misbehaviour and foul language, or we are not serious. It's time to shit or get off the pot'.

A murmur of approval sounded for these remarks even if they took exception to the man's crudity of expression. Standards of student behaviour had been deteriorating at an alarming rate.
Corrigan was the man to present the plain unvarnished truth, albeit in unparliamentary language.
Miss Hayes, the Religious Education teacher, was anxious to come to the aid of the principal in the face of such an onslaught.
'I accept that there are problems of indiscipline that have to be addressed. However, I feel that we all have a responsibility to inculcate proper Christian values'.
Miss Hayes delivered her message with her trademark blend of sincerity and naivety.
Stephen had identified a group of teachers opposed to Lynch and his methods. Jimmy Corrigan was the principal's most vocal critic at such meetings.
The group, more favourably disposed towards the principal, were known as The Lynch Mob. Miss Hayes featured in that section of staff. It was significant that these people now found themselves in the minority on the staff.
Corrigan reacted to Miss Hayes's contribution.
Getting to his feet as he spoke, he was passionate in his tone.
'That is precisely the thinking that has us where we are today. These boys must be taught respect and discipline, but that won't be achieved in discussion groups in a Religion class or with the likes of me breaking up a Maths class to teach them manners. Rules are rules, and

management must enforce those rules for everyone, including the lads from the posh areas.'

He sat down to the sound of applause ringing in his ears.

Jimmy could always be relied on to say what needed to be said.

Simon Lynch received some sympathetic and reassuring contributions from certain staff members who appreciated his invidious position. This heated discussion continued for over an hour, with many contributions coming from the floor.

After the debate on discipline, attention turned to the upcoming Parent/Teacher meeting and the annual talent competition. Nothing was without its controversy. Towards the end of the session, Mr Lynch asked for volunteers to supervise the afternoon's study hall. Parents had been assured that such a facility would be made available after the staff meeting. It would look good to the parents.

For teachers unwilling to volunteer, it was a time to keep one's head down. Those in the principal's line of sight needed to be very agreeable or else be possessed of nerves of steel if they were to face down the pressure of the Lynch stare.

The final business involved the setting of times for the various department meetings. By now, there was the inevitable shuffling of chairs and papers associated with the conclusion of a session. Stephen heard through the din that the teachers in the English department would meet after school the following day.

Simon Lynch was on his feet attempting to fill in the remaining time slots.

'Right then, and at what time will the meeting be for those working with the slow learners?'
Lynch had not yet got his head around the current terminology on such matters.
'When the big hand is at six and the small hand is at four,' came a suggestion from the back of the room.
The meeting finally over, Simon Lynch breathed a sigh of relief. As principal, he looked forward to staff meetings almost as much as he looked forward to a prostate examination. He concluded by reminding the staff that the annual Mass for First-Year students and their parents would be held in the college oratory the following night, with the usual refreshments being served afterwards.

As the day was still young, Tom suggested to Stephen that they should take a trip out to the golf course in Ardbeg. Stephen, who had never held a golf club in his life, much less own a set of them, protested that the trip would be a waste of time and money under such circumstances.
'Not at all, I'm useless at it too, but it will be a bit of craic. I was out here with Seamus last week, and we belted around for a while.'
'That's all very well, but what are we going to use for clubs?' wondered Stephen.
'That's no problem. Seamus said that I could borrow his any time. You can bring Frank's club'.
'I'd have to give him a shout at the bank first', he thought,
'You must be daft. You're only borrowing them after all, not bloody-well robbing them. And anyway, he wouldn't thank you for annoying him at work.'
Tom certainly had a point there, so Stephen agreed to help himself to the clubs. They loaded both sets into Tom's rickety *Toyota Starlet* and headed for Ardbeg.

The feeling of being free when one might ordinarily be locked up is most pleasurable. As the two men sped out of Castlehome, they knew from their timetables where they would usually be at this time. This knowledge, in no small way, contributed to the feeling of delight. To Stephen Daly, outings such as these acted as a sort of safety valve for him.
'Maybe this teaching lark has something to recommend it after all', laughed Stephen.

Tom had a tape of Elton John playing at full volume. He roared the words along with the singer.

♫*But your candle burned out long before your legend ever did*♫

'It's hard to think poor Princess Di is dead, 'Tom said, interrupting his singing.

Stephen agreed.

'And she was killed in a speeding car, so take your fucking time. The evening is long'

Both agreed that the song would be forever associated with Diana rather than Marilyn Monroe, its original inspiration.

'That Marilyn must have been some bird all the same', mused Stephen.

'She must have been'. Tom accepted.

'But on the subject of fine birds, how are you getting along with Sinead?'

'Has she fallen for your seductive charms yet?'

'I slept with her last night'.

Stephen attempted to keep a straight face.

'You did in my arse. I heard you coming in, and you were very early at that. Did Sinead send you packing?'

Stephen laughed aloud at this question even though it could be interpreted as being a slight on him. He eventually confided in Tom that he had not asked her out yet, but he was working up to it. Tom advised caution as regards Sinead but hinted that Pamela might be a better bet for him.

Stephen pretended not to hear and continued to hum with the song.

After twenty minutes of driving, the boys arrived in Ardbeg. It was nothing like Stephen had imagined. He had been to watch the Irish Open once and had expected something smaller definitely but certainly along similar lines. Instead, what he saw was neglected fields with sheep grazing in them.

'Greenkeepers in woolly jumpers', joked Stephen.

'Bet you never saw a course like this in Dublin? Tom queried.

Stephen readily admitted that he had not.

'And I bet that you never got green fees at a fiver a group either, or had the course to yourself', Tom added with much pride in his adopted town.

Tom was right. Apart from them, there was not another living soul to be seen on the course. Work was certainly the curse of the golfing classes.

A corrugated iron shed served as the clubhouse. Green fees were posted in the box provided. The people here obviously operated on trust.

Tom and Stephen presented an unlikely appearance on any golf course. They both wore anoraks as protection against the harsh breeze, with Tom sporting a pair of wellington boots. After a few minutes on the course, Stephen saw the wisdom of bringing such footwear, as some sections were no better than a swamp.

Stephen joined in the play, but his game left much to be desired.

'Looks a lot easier on television, doesn't it?' ventured Stephen.

A frustrated looking Tom agreed.

'It sure does'.

Stephen hit his next ball out of bounds.

To retrieve his ball, Stephen leapt up on the wall alongside the wire fence.

Casually, throwing one leg over the wire, he was oblivious to the danger involved. Tom, who had been considering his next shot, heard Stephen emit a pitiful roar. He looked around to see an ashen-faced Stephen, holding his crotch in agony.

'You never told me that it was a bloody electric fence', he moaned.

'I didn't know, Stephen but thanks for telling me. I don't want to be hitting too many high notes tonight,' he joked.

'Fuck you and your voice, help me down out of here before my balls are fried'.

A jeering Tom gingerly assisted Stephen to the ground.

'Look on the bright side, that surge of power might be just what you needed in that department. After all, you could do with all the help you get.'

It took Stephen a good ten minutes before he could stand properly and throw any sort of shape at restarting the game. Within the last half hour, others had arrived on the course.

Tom waved through two ladies, who were coming up rather quickly behind them

'We'll let you through ladies, my friend here is having a problem locating his balls'.

The ladies graciously acknowledged the courtesy and passed on through, leaving Stephen with little choice but to smile benevolently at them.

'Did you have to say that, Tom? What sort of eejit must I appear to them?'
'Will you stop moaning, Daly. Sure no one here knows you from a rook out here'.
Over the remaining holes, the boys' standard of play did not noticeably improve. On the contrary, they spent more time with their backsides sticking out of ditches, searching for lost balls than they spent on the course.
'No bloody use having cheap green fees if we are out a fortune on golf balls', Tom sighed, echoing what Stephen himself was thinking.
They soon became aware of some people on the previous green who seemed to be shouting and waving a golf club at them.
'They can't be shouting at us because we know nobody here, and we didn't do anything to annoy anybody'.
The two decided that, all things considered, it was best to ignore the shouting and carry on playing.
'Probably some local idiots, high on magic mushrooms or maybe another bloke, who got himself stuck on the electric fence', laughed Tom.

A few moments later, they observed a middle-aged man racing breathlessly towards them. He was brandishing a golf club.
'Jaysus, what in the hell have we done, Tom?' wondered Stephen, the anxiety growing within him.
In a moment, the strange and fearsome figure was standing alongside them.
'Are you two fucking deaf or hard of hearing or just plain stupid?'

The boys just looked at each other.
None of the three options given in the question seemed appealing.
'Didn't ye hear me shouting from back there?'
'I found this golf club near the last green. I presume it belongs to one of you, but you clearly couldn't care less about it."

Stephen immediately recalled dropping the 9 iron. What with the electric shock and all, his concentration was not what it should be. He thanked the man profusely and apologised for the bother he had put him to.
'Wow, I'm glad of that. Frank would have had my guts for garters, especially as I never even asked him to borrow his clubs in the first place'.
The would-be golfers headed home after twelve holes deciding that perhaps it was better to stick to the day jobs. They had an evening meal to prepare and then the night in Taylor's ahead of them.

The pub was quiet as the two young teachers made their entrance. The few customers present were engaged in quiet conversation or sipping solitary drinks as they scanned the latest edition of the *Castlehome News*.

The barman, Gerry, welcomed the boys and immediately set about pulling two pints of *Guinness*. Tom was a familiar face in the pub and was the resident musical performer.

On this point, Gerry was mischievous. He constantly reminded Tom that it was merely a case of the customers tolerating him. Stephen was a less frequent visitor but was still a familiar face in the establishment.

As the three chatted at the bar, Andy Flanagan joined the conversation. He was arguably the best customer that Taylor's had. Some viewed him as a bit of a character. In contrast, others saw him as being an opinionated ignoramus. Stephen had spoken to him briefly on another occasion. He had a grown-up family and had been a widower for the previous five years. Whenever Gerry was slow or negligent in providing him with a refill, Andy would demand preferential treatment, insisting that his custom was paying the staff wages. He was probably right.

'What did ye make of Ardbeg then? I hear ye were out there', asked Andy by way of a conversation opener.

Tom could not resist the temptation.

'It's an unusual set-up, right enough. I had been out there before and knew what to expect. However, poor Stephen got quite a shock'.

Tom laughed heartily at his own joke. Andy was not impressed.

'God, deliver me from these fools,' he hissed, turning his back on them.

'It's just a private joke, Andy. I wouldn't take any notice'.

Andy resumed his earlier position and began to air his entrenched opinion.

'I don't know what they want spending money, building golf courses like that for. Sure, that's only for doctors or lawyers or people like ye, that have too much time on their hands'.

Andy had issues with much of what he observed in contemporary Ireland.

'That's another thing too. Young people have no respect anymore. When I was a young boy, we were taught to respect our elders. Nowadays, it's all about educating people whether they want it or can even benefit from it. If a lad had brains in my day, he stayed on at school. If he hadn't, well then, the parents took him out of school and got a trade for him or put him into a shop. Nowadays, I see big lumps of fellas in school uniforms, heading up to ye in the morning, smoking cigarettes and chatting up the convent girls. I'd swear the same buckos wouldn't know what a day's work is like,' he fumed.

'True for you', said Tom.

Stephen zoned out of the conversation as soon as he noticed Sinead enter the bar in the company of Pamela. In a moment, Tom had seen them too. He shouted a greeting to the girls and invited them to join them at the bar. He hoped that he might stir things up for Stephen and get a bit of craic going.

Pamela was delighted to accept the gift of flowers, which Stephen had delivered to her. She saw it as an encouraging sign for her.

'Thanks for the lovely bouquet. It was a lovely surprise. There was really no need.'

'Well, you did prepare a lovely meal'.

'Well, it was my pleasure. We must do it again sometime'.

Stephen was not so sure but said nothing.

Andy disapproved of such unmanly behaviour. Men had changed a great deal over the years. He was also struck by the contrast between teachers in his day and the current crop.

'In my day, we never had a schoolmistress the likes of you. No, we had a right old witch with a sour puss on her, who would frighten dogs away from your gate. We wouldn't bring milk to school in case she'd turn it sour'.

As Pamela looked as if she was tired of his contributions, Andy turned his attention to Sinead.

'And what useless thing might you be teaching now, young lassie?'

Then, casting him a contemptuous side-glance, Sinead brusquely informed him that she was not a teacher but rather a nurse.

'Are you now? In the Regional, is it?'

'Yeah, why?'

'Are you working in a male or female ward'?

'It's not divided like that anymore', she scornfully responded.

Sinead could never be accused of suffering fools gladly.

'Holy God, mixed wards, whatever next?' Andy asked in disbelief.

'But tell me, girl, there was a neighbour man, Tommy Joe Smith admitted there yesterday. I was wondering if he had the operation yet.'

Sinead thought for a moment as the name sounded vaguely familiar.

'What was the nature of his illness?'
'Ah, it was just a bit of bother with his waterworks. Prostate, I think they call it', he said. He was embarrassed to refer to such an intimate part of his friend's anatomy in the young female's presence.
Sinead soon recollected his old neighbour.
'I don't really know anything about him. Even if I did, I couldn't speak about it.'
Andy had to respect that. Nevertheless, he still managed to inject a barbed retort.
'I know exactly the *Official Secrets Act* and all that.'

Sinead was stung by that remark. But, then, she saw her chance and went for it with zest, fully determined to shut him up for the remainder of the night.
'That can be a particular problem with men of your age. You know men don't pay half enough attention to their welfare in that area. I could, if you like, get you some information leaflets on the subject'.
Andy assured her that everything was all right with his waterworks. Then, as if to underline it, he excused himself and headed for the toilets.
'That's an early sign', Sinead informed him as he turned the corner.
'What's that?' He asked.
'Going too often', she whispered loudly as the old man disdainfully turned his back on her.
'I don't think we'll be bothered with him again', Tom predicted as he readied his guitar for his musical slot.

Stephen was now sitting down at a corner table with the two girls. Pamela seemed to be especially pleasant to him. She must have thanked him for the flowers at least three times. Even Sinead was also very civil towards him. He was impressed by how she could handle herself. She would make a formidable opponent.

For the next hour or so, Stephen chatted, in a very relaxed and easy fashion, to both women. He would have loved to get Sinead alone but didn't know how he could engineer that. He had already decided against formally asking her out, at least to start with anyway.

His strategy was to casually ask her along to some random event and make it appear a spur of the moment thing. If she declined, then there would be no loss of face. If she agreed, it would be as effective as a gold plated invitation, accompanied by a fanfare of royal trumpeters. So, his initial challenge was to prise her away from Pamela to get an opportunity to ask her.

Pamela casually mentioned that she was going home to Mullingar for the weekend to mark the silver jubilee of her parents' wedding. God certainly moves in mysterious ways.

This information was music to Stephen's ears. There was now an opportunity.

Saturday night would tell the story.

He declined the girls' invitation to partake in a late-night cup of coffee. There would be plenty of time for that. He had to go home and plan his strategy.

Dealing with the Fourth Year English class was the bane of Stephen Daly's life. They were as great a collection of lazy individuals as one would find this side of the Urals. Academic ineptitude was something they could not be held responsible for. However, their behaviour was another matter. Stephen would have settled for just a little in the way of courtesy or respect.

These were Ordinary Level students. If there had existed such a thing then as a Foundation course at Leaving Cert. level, most of this crew would have opted to take that option. Nine or ten of the class were as well mannered and respectful as would be possible to find in this age group. Unfortunately, in such circumstances, it is the lowest common denominator that generally prevails.

The students were in the room before Stephen arrived. Presumably, some long-suffering teacher had released them prematurely. Stephen took a deep breath outside before he opened the door. The scene that presented itself to him was nearly enough to make him cry out with helplessness. He observed a boy kicking a football out of his hands, at full force towards the blackboard, which doubled as the goalposts. Another ruffian was holding a classmate dangling by the heels from the window of that second-floor room. Stephen roared for order at the top of his voice as he ran for the students at the window.

'Only messing, Sir,' was the familiar refrain from the perpetrator of this most dangerous variety of horseplay. He decided to send this thrill-seeker and the indoor Gaelic footballer to the principal.

None of this was an ideal introduction to the Romantic Poet, John Keats.

Today Stephen was going to introduce these boys to the aesthetic pleasures of that delicate soul's poetry. He set the scene as effectively as possible, alluding to the poet's tender age, terminal illness, and his love of the woman in his life. Despite the interruptions, Stephen had a course to cover, even though it seemed the most inappropriate material for this group.

He attempted to explain the poem by stanza with particular emphasis on mood and the trademark sensuous description. He then asked if there were any questions. A hand shot up.

'Sir, are we getting a half-day next Friday?'

'Questions on the poem or the poet only', roared Stephen.

Two students at the back swapped punches in another mock argument. Stephen directed both of them to stand outside the door and continued as well as he could.

He asked the boys to take out their copybooks as he was going to give them an explanation of the technical terms used in the poem.

'Sir, I can't write this, I have forgotten my copy book',

'Has anyone got a spare pen for me?'

A duel in high fielding inevitably ensued as the requested pen was flung from the far end of the classroom.

Towards the end of class, he assigned the homework. The voices again pleaded inability.

'I can't do it. I have a sore hand, Sir.'

'I don't have the poetry book yet Sir, my mother is getting it next week.'

A cheeky bastard interrupted.

'From what I hear, she's getting it every night.'

'Shut up, you little prick. Your mother's a scrubber.'

Stephen greeted the bell for the end of class as a punched out boxer greets the bell for the contest's end.

At the eleven o'clock break, the principal approached Stephen solemnly.

'I interviewed those two boys. It's a very serious situation. They should never have been allowed into that room on their own. You should know that boys will be boys. And by the way, Stephen, it's not a good idea to put them outside the door. There is an insurance issue. You know what I mean.'

He had not left them alone in the room. He was about to explain, but Lynch did not wait for a reaction. Instead, he proceeded to the door rattling his keys in a not too subtle hint to teachers to get back to class on time.

Stephen was experiencing a baptism of fire. Nobody said that it was going to be easy for the first year. However, he had no idea that it was going to be quite as difficult as it was. Doubts were beginning to cross his mind. Maybe he was not cut out to be a teacher. He knew that this was not the case. He enjoyed teaching. The trouble was he rarely got a chance to teach. It was generally a case of crowd control.

Stephen constantly felt under pressure. His social life had acted as a safety valve, through which the stresses of the job found some release.

So, it seemed somehow appropriate that he had his eye on a nurse as a prospective girlfriend. He certainly would need a large measure of her tender, loving care.

He was looking forward to seeing his family again, if only briefly. They had maintained their twice or thrice weekly contact with him. He continued to keep up the pretence that everything was fine. In reality, it was anything but fine.

His reputation as a teacher had hit rock bottom. There was precious little chance of salvaging it. While his social life could be considered full and varied, he was far from happy. His pride had taken a severe blow. He was disappointed at the way that he was drinking most of his disposable income. He was also disappointed that the girl he had set his sights on was still not on his arm.

Nevertheless, he would keep up a good front for the family. Castlehome might still deliver the goods for Stephen Daly. If only he knew what lay around the corner for him.

On the night of the annual First-Year Mass, the school was looking its splendid best. For many parents, this was their first real chance to view the place. Windows, which had not been cleaned in months, were again transparent. Fresh paint had been applied to mud-stained walls. Student artwork bedecked the lobby area with air freshener liberally used anywhere within a hundred-yard radius of a toilet. The oratory itself was at its most beautiful, with the altar tastefully adorned with greenery. The Superior of the order, Rev. Michael Sweeney, former President of St. Jude's, was the celebrant.

Tom and Stephen had arrived ahead of schedule as they were helping with preparations. Seats and tables were borrowed from the gymnasium and study hall to the old parlour, where the refreshments would be served after the Mass.

It was then that Stephen Daly's eye was attracted to someone whose appearance completely captivated him. This stunning, older woman oozed sex appeal through every pore of her finely chiselled body. If she were single and twenty years younger, she would be the woman of his dreams, whom he would pursue to the ends of the earth.

He had no idea who this vision was but understandably presumed that she was a parent of one of the college's first-year students. Stephen envied whoever was lucky enough to be the man in her life. The lady had to be about forty-five years of age but was amazingly youthful in appearance. She was incredibly beautiful, tall with shoulder-length black hair and a really pleasant, smiling face. A body-hugging, black knee-length dress accentuated her athletic figure.

He was determined to discover her identity. Surely one of the other teachers would know who she was.
As it happened, he did not have to ask anyone at all.
'I see Lynch's wife has graced us with her presence again', remarked Tom as he observed his mate follow her with his eyes.
'I can never figure what she ever saw in that bastard.'
Stephen could not believe what he was hearing.
'I don't believe you. Are you seriously telling me that Lynch is married to that stunner?'
'Yes, Stephen, incredible as it may seem, she is married to our Wally of a principal'.
For the very first time, Stephen envied Lynch.
'Imagine going home to that every evening! It's a wonder the bastard shows up at all in the morning', Tom reckoned.
'Tom, have you ever been talking to her?'
'Yea, we all have. The woman is good craic, unlike her husband. Eva is what she insists on being called. She wants none of this Mrs Lynch stuff'.
Stephen was open-mouthed in sheer disbelief.
'But what's she doing with him? I mean, she's a real beauty, and he's such a miserable bastard, not to mention being twenty years older. He is a dirty old ram.'
His eyes followed Eva as she chatted smilingly to staff and parents alike. Everyone seemed to know and like her. Her eyes momentarily met his. Stephen looked away in embarrassment. He hoped that she had noticed that he had been staring at her. Unknown to Stephen, Eva

had already noticed him. She had seen him even before he had laid eyes on her, and she fully intended to make his acquaintance.
Meanwhile, Stephen was still attempting to make sense of their union.
'Were men scarce back then or what?'
Tom could easily recall that he was similarly shocked when he first met her. There was certainly no way one would put them together.
'I don't know what the story was', Tom admitted.
'Maybe he had her up the pole, but then again, it's hard to imagine Simon getting his lad out at all. Who knows? Maybe it was a love match. Did you ever think of that, Stephen?' Tom remarked sagely but unconvincingly.
'No, I wouldn't have thought so. Tell me, have they any kids?' Stephen wondered aloud.
'They have twin girls. Wasn't Lynch boasting about how well they did in the Junior Cert. I think they are boarding in some posh school'.
There was certainly no accounting for Eva's taste.
So, old Simon removed the academic gown occasionally. He tried to imagine them having sexual relations but was getting more nauseous at the notion.
The celebrant was skilled at adapting his message to suit his audience. He could be serious when he felt the need and appropriately light-hearted at other times. Tonight, he was in an expansive mood. He reminisced about his time at the college and how he still missed the classroom.
'The bloody hypocrite', thought Stephen. 'He was probably doing novenas to get out of this madhouse.'

After Mass, the guests made their way to the old parlour to enjoy some light refreshments. As was the norm on such school occasions, the female staff poured cups of tepid tea and coffee into polystyrene cups. An impressive array of pastries, tarts and sandwiches adorned the side tables.

It was a case of all smiles between parents and teachers. Some of the more experienced teachers who were veterans of many skirmishes at Parent/Teacher meetings kept a respectable distance. Teachers were fine as long as they had nothing negative to say about their children. Those affable and smiling parents might quickly show their teeth. In the circumstances, cold civility tempered with a hint of aloofness seemed the best approach to adopt.

There followed a minimum degree of mingling. Stephen momentarily found himself standing alone along the back wall of the room. As he sipped from his cup of stewed tea, he was considering nipping down to Taylor's when a gentle tap on his arm startled him. He was practically rendered speechless as he found himself gazing into the smiling face of the woman he had been staring at all night. After a moment of self-conscious speechlessness, he eventually managed to utter a surprised acknowledgement.

'Ah, Mrs Lynch, isn't it,' he stuttered.

'Please call me, Eva; everyone does', she said softly, taking his right hand and shaking it gently.

For a very perceptible moment, she held his hand in hers.

The nature of her approach had wrong-footed Stephen.

'I am afraid that you have the advantage on me', she continued, her eyes all the time scrutinising his face.
Stephen was all apologies.
'Sorry, I'm Stephen Daly. I'm new here. I teach English'.
Stephen felt nervous in case her husband had told her about his poor performance. Old Simon had probably told her about the bare ass in the door as well. Stephen didn't want her to think that he was an inglorious failure.
He attempted to banish such negative thoughts and try to act as any normal teacher would in the presence of the principal's wife. He hated being caught off-guard like this even though she seemed a very pleasant and agreeable sort.
'I hope your husband had nothing bad to say about me'.
Mrs Lynch seemed to pick up on his insecurity and seemed keen to exploit it.
'Oh! You mean to tell me that I am talking to a bold boy'.
There was mischief in her smile and a delightful twinkle in those pretty brown eyes as she surveyed St. Jude's latest recruit.
Having already sensed Stephen's concern regarding her husband's comment, she reassured him that she had heard nothing.
She frequently touched his hand during their short conversation, allowing her touch to linger for that extra moment. It felt as if it was more than just physically reinforcing her points. For Stephen, this was something satisfying yet incredibly disarming.
Eva was standing very close to him, tantalisingly, encroaching on his personal space. Ordinarily, getting up close and personal to such a

good-looking woman was something he would have given his eye teeth for. However, in the company of this older, most exquisite woman, he felt juvenile and immature. This was unchartered territory. No woman had ever had this effect on him. It was as if her presence had robbed him of his intellectual capacity and turned him into a blathering fool.

He could feel his face turning red. The room was becoming much too warm for him. His heart was pounding so loudly that it felt as if its intemperate beat was audible, even to the woman. Perspiration was threatening to break out all over his body. His breath came much too quickly, ending any faint hope of maintaining a composed facade.

He knew full well that in a few hours, he would be replaying this scene over again in his mind, chastising himself for his puerile reactions. But right now, he was floundering. The older woman had captivated him. He may not have recognised it yet, but he was already under her spell.

Eva Lynch made polite conversation about his life in Dublin. She also enquired about the nature of the social scene in Castlehome. Still, even as she spoke, the sound of her voice was becoming distant and faint. He answered her questions in a very nervous and agitated fashion.

He was greatly embarrassed when she asked whether he had met any attractive girls in Castlehome since his arrival. It was a bit like one's auntie asking whether you had a girlfriend or not.

Stephen hesitated. He felt distinctly uncomfortable on the topic of the fairer sex. He needed to escape from this situation. Jimmy Corrigan unwittingly provided that means of escape.

Jimmy's voice, when he spoke, shook him. It was like being awakened from a dream by a particularly shrill alarm clock. He looked at his colleague like he might at a stranger, who had shouted at him from a crowd.

Corrigan, it seemed, had been nipping off early but was frustrated in his efforts by a flat battery. He needed a push.

'I'm sorry to interrupt you, Eva. I need Stephen to give my car a push. The bloody battery is dead.'

Stephen was only too glad to excuse himself and walk out into the fresh air to the back car park.

The cool air and the misty rain quickly helped Stephen recover his composure.

Corrigan was mildly curious to know what Eva had been saying. He had also sensed the young lad's discomfort.

'You looked under pressure there, lad. Was she looking for some young blood or what?'

Stephen was in no mood for this line of talk.

'As a matter of fact, Jimmy, she was asking me if you were still as big a bollocks as ever'.

Jimmy laughed heartily at this, but he was undeterred.

'Did she mention Simon at all? I doubt if he's up to the job. That one would wear out a man half his age.'

'Jimmy, I told her that you'd oblige if Simon ever fell down on the job.'

Stephen continued on, giving Jimmy a firm pat on the back.
'Stephen, I know my limitations. That one would laugh at my best effort.'
'Sure, what is so different about her. Isn't she a woman after all?'
Stephen wondered, anxious not to appear too interested in learning about her.
Corrigan had an interesting way of looking at the matter.
'Women are a bit like cars. Most are standard, economy models but there some high-end models that are expensive to run and maintain. Eva Lynch would be one of those high spec women'.
Stephen thought it better to let the matter drop.
'Right then, I'll give your standard model a push and then you can give me a lift home. I think I'll give the pub a miss tonight.'
'So, you're not going back to Eva Peron in there?'
'You must be joking. A high-spec woman like her and I only an innocent young fellow!
'Wise fucking man!'
At least, he was not the same pitiful idiot when it came to talking to Sinead. It was high time to make his move on her. Like an army general, he would have his strategy well worked out. He hoped that it would prove to be a successful strategy. Sinead was worthy of his best endeavours.

Stephen had given great consideration to his game plan. On Saturday night, a table quiz was scheduled for *Castlehome and District Tennis Club* to raise funds for the major court-resurfacing project.
He was not a member of the tennis club. The game held little attraction for him but housemates Seamus and Frank were members. Indeed, Seamus was this year's club treasurer. The lads were doing their *rent-a-crowd* job for the night.

Tom Clarke had also been asked to provide the music after the quiz finished. The music would help create a bit of an atmosphere to tempt the crowd to spend money in the bar afterwards.

For the quiz, there would be teams of four people. Stephen had it all worked through meticulously. Tom, Frank, and he would be on the same team. Being a committee member, Seamus would have organisational duties on the night, leaving one place to fill. With Pamela gone home for her parents' anniversary celebrations and Susan, the other housemate working on night duty, it left one obvious candidate. Sinead would be finished work at eight, in plenty of time to be changed and ready for the nine-thirty start. That is if he could convince her to attend.
Everything was falling into place very neatly as if fate had ordained him to be with Sinead this weekend
Stephen had confidently looked further down the road, past the actual quiz. He was confident that he and Sinead would be thrown together without any very obvious manoeuvring on his part. Tom would be busy performing his musical duties. Frank would presumably move

away to chat with his tennis buddies. That would leave just himself alone with the ravishing Sinead.

At about ten o'clock on Friday evening, he telephoned the object of his desire. He invited her to join the dream team. She was on her way out to meet with a colleague when he called. He attempted to sound as casual as possible.

'The bank lads are organising a table quiz in the Tennis Club on Saturday night. They want as many teams as possible. Frank, Tom and I are on one team. However, we need a fourth person. We would like you to join us.'

It was not something that interested Sinead at all.

'What's wrong with Seamus? Is he out of town or what?' she asked.

'No, he's involved in the organisation. He will be marking sheets and the like'.

Sinead was not very keen.

'Quizzes are not my thing'.

'Ah, come on. I'm banking on you, Sinead'.

'I don't know, Stephen. I'm no good at general knowledge. Anyway, I'd be too nervous to answer'.

'Ah, no Sinead, there is no answering out at all. It's like a written quiz. The team talks it over and agree on an answer. Come on; it should be a bit of a laugh. Tom is doing a bit of singing afterwards. Now, if that puts you off, I can fully understand'.

She laughed.

'No, I think I have developed an immunity to his singing by now'.

'That doesn't sound too bad then. But I warn you. I'll be no addition to the team'.

That mattered little to Stephen.

The arrangements were made.

'I'll drop over, and we will ring for a taxi. You will be able to have a drink without worrying about the car'.

'I'll see you tomorrow so. Enjoy the rest of your evening'.

He hoped that he would be brave enough to see his plan through. He feared that he might be like a dog, constantly chasing cars with no idea what to do if he caught one.

On Saturday night, Stephen arrived at Number 22, The Manor, where Sinead was just applying the last of her make-up. She was a vision in a peach-coloured top and snow-white jeans. Stephen would have probably considered her outfit to be sexy even if she was draped in a moth-eaten, army blanket.

He excused him and proceeded to ring the taxi company. As he spoke, he caught Sinead's reflection in the hall mirror, combing her beautiful dark tresses and checking her make-up. He liked to imagine that this was to look good for him.

After a few moments, the taxi arrived and they were on their way. Unfortunately, Stephen had precious little time to converse with her on the short trip to the pavilion at Castlehome Tennis Club. He hoped that he would have more time to chat her up later in the night.

At the bar, there was a great hum of conversation. They would make up Table 25. All that had to be done now was to pay the fee and get the drinks in.

'The first round tonight will be on *General Knowledge'.* The smooth-talking quizmaster informed them.

'General Knowledge, is that the top army bloke?' joked Sinead.

From the outset, it was clear that most teams were not taking the evening's contest seriously, with one or two obvious exceptions. People were there for the craic and were not overly competitive. A succession of humorous responses was greeted with hilarity. Answers were shouted aloud. There was considerable sharing or trading of information between certain tables.

There were, however, the travelling teams of 'Quiz Pros.' as they called them. These were carefully constituted teams comprised of people with the appropriate specialist information plus a wide spattering of general knowledge. They researched their material and did their homework assiduously in an attempt to emerge as victors.

These rather sad individuals were treated with a mixture of disdain and sympathy by the rest of the participants.

What was the real name of the Wild West hero popularly known as Buffalo Bill?

Tom suggested 'Simon Lynch' to the great amusement of Stephen.

Sinead, who had taken on the evening's writing duties, surprised everybody by knowing that the legend's name was Cody. She had a good explanation.

'My uncle has the same name. It's funny how he was nicknamed Buffalo Bill from the first day he went to school. Anyway, I encountered a lot of cowboys in my time.'

Stephen's tongue had responded before he had engaged his brain.

'All of them anxious for a ride, no doubt'.

There was shocked laughter at the table. However, Stephen suspected that he had ruined his chances with Sinead. After all his meticulous planning, he would have kicked his arse back to Dublin if such a vulgar remark were to scupper his chances with Sinead.

Luckily she saw the funny side and had not taken offence.

What is the unit of currency of Panama?

Frank, who had often worked in Foreign Exchange, did not know.

Apart from the canal, Stephen had only ever heard Panama mentioned in connection with headgear. For that reason, he offered the Hat as a possible answer.

The next question was about *Sport.* Tom, a passionate Manchester United supporter, effortlessly named the United manager when they won the European Cup in the sixties.

By the halfway stage, Table 25 had moved into a very respectable joint third position.

It was all to play for.

Despite the unorthodox manner in which the team had been constructed, it was quite well balanced. Stephen was more than adequate on literature and current affairs. Sinead was a film and T.V. buff. As would be expected, she scored full points on all questions about Science. Tom knew plenty about Modern Music and even more about Sport. Frank's evenings spent watching the History Channel did not go to waste either. Better still, all four were enjoying themselves. Stephen took particular pleasure in noting Sinead's enjoyment of the proceedings.

During the interval, Tom got refills for everybody from the bar.

'You have to keep the brain well oiled', he joked as he placed the full glasses on the table.

Stephen felt the need to visit the toilets.

A fellow urinal user was more than a little consumed by the quiz bug. He waylaid Stephen and insisted on reciting the Tudor kings and queens of England to him and the names of the last five Irish Greyhound Derby winners. This ability was all a very impressive feat. Stephen, however, had little interest in such trivia.

Being unsure of the name of one particular champion greyhound, the quiz buff stopped for thought. Stephen conveniently excused himself, but not before pointing out to his erudite friend that he was peeing onto his own shoes. Stephen Daly resumed his position as the second half of the quiz commenced. The pattern was much the same as earlier, with a succession of hilarious answers being offered.

At the end of the quiz, the final tally was completed on the score sheets. Table 25 had finished in second place. Again, a team of table quiz professionals had taken a commanding lead and were not to be caught.

The four mates were delighted and engaged in a well-deserved bout of self-congratulation even though the second prize was little more than an excuse.

Still, it would buy a few drinks.

Tom was already tuning up for his musical performance. Frank, as would be expected, went off to mingle.

Stephen finally found himself all alone with the lovely Sinead. He could not have planned it better.

'That was a bit of craic', said Sinead as she moved closer to Stephen at the table.

'I enjoyed having you here.'

He hoped that he did not sound too infatuated.

'The way you answered tonight, I might be calling on you again'.

He waited to see what response this might elicit.

'The questions just suited me', she answered in a voice that gave little away.

With Pamela back on Monday, it could well be weeks before Stephen got to this stage again. Sinead certainly seemed relaxed and easy in his company, nothing like the brash girl he had met earlier. This change might have been an encouraging sign, or conversely, it may just have indicated total indifference on her part.'

He needed to get clarity on this point.

'I never knew you were so good at films. Do you go to the cinema much?'

As soon as he had the words uttered, Stephen could have kicked himself again.
He might as well have asked:
'Do you come here often?
'Not as often as I would like to,' she answered.
'I frequently go with my old school friends when I'm home in Tralee. However, the girls aren't particularly interested', confided Sinead.
'And of course, the boyfriend can't come to Castlehome too often'? Stephen asked, determined to force the issue, whether for good or ill.
Sinead smiled coyly but made him none the wiser as regards any romantic involvement on her part.
Stephen gritted his teeth and decided to bite the bullet.
'Well then, how's about you and me hitting the movies together some night?'
Despite the butterflies in his stomach, he tried desperately to make it sound like a casual and spontaneous invitation. He would hate to be knocked back, especially after what appeared to be a successful first outing.
'Sounds good to me', replied Sinead in the matter of fact manner he had striven to emulate.
Although he was delighted with the positive response, he was nevertheless worried. He was unsure how Sinead had interpreted this invitation.
He now wondered whether she viewed it as a valid date or simply as two people, at a loose end, going to the cinema together. Her calm, unemotional response betrayed no clues. Stephen felt sure that she

would have made the same response if he had agreed to lend her a book.
'What evening would suit you?' Stephen wanted to pin her down to a firm arrangement. The last thing he wanted was to have to go through all the preliminaries again at a later date. Don't leave the job half-done, he urged himself.
'There's a change of programme in the *Odeon* on Wednesday. So, I'm off that night if that suits', she answered in the same unemotional tone.
"That's perfect; I'll call for you,' he added.
Stephen observed his learned friend from the urinals shuffling up to him.
He proudly announced that he had finally recalled the Derby winner's name, which had earlier slipped his mind.
Stephen thanked him and proclaimed himself indebted to him for this information.
He also expressed the hope that the man's shoes would dry out soon.
'Who's that weirdo?' Sinead asked.
'Just someone I was chatting to in the jacks'.
Sinead's eyes were opened wide with incomprehension at this exchange. So this was what men got up to in the lavatories. And all the chat men have about women going to the toilets in pairs.
But, if it was Stephen's lucky night, it was not so for Tom. No one was passing the slightest attention to him or his music. He might as well have been picking his nose in the corner as guitar picking in that company. In the aftermath of the quiz, the people there just wanted to talk and socialise.

'Bastards!' fumed Tom.

'It's the last fucking night I'm coming out here. They haven't even the manners to listen. What you expect anyway from the jumped up crowd of pricks. Tennis Club, my arse! They are a shower of pretentious pricks'.

Sinead feigned sympathy.

'Poor you, up there, suffering for your art!'

'Can we get a seat back with you, Tom?' Stephen asked.

"You can; if you come now, I better go before I do something I might regret.

Having brought Sinead home, Stephen was disappointed that she had not invited him in for a nightcap. Yet, he was thrilled at the prospect of the upcoming date with her.

He proudly announced to his surprised companion.

'Tom, I'm in there with Sinead.'

Seeing his friend's sceptical expression, he continued.

'I swear I am, honest to God. She has agreed to come on a date with me'.

His companion was more than a little surprised.

'Well, I didn't see much sign of it back there. Are you sure you didn't have one too many tonight?'

'No, it's true. Wednesday night at the flicks!'

The back row of the movies! Yea, I'm definitely in there, Tom'.

Realising that one is underperforming in one's job is demoralising. It is nothing short of humiliating when other people voice that reality. It is even worse when there is a designated day for them to do so. The first Parent/Teacher meeting of his career had not gone well. Some of the more angry parents charged him with being an incompetent teacher. Even worse was the look of sympathy in the eyes of some mothers who assured him that things might yet work out for him.

The principal had encouraged all teachers to be positive in their reports and send them away happy.

'To you, some of these lads might be lazy and bad-mannered but don't forget that every mother's goose is a swan. Please be sensitive with your comments'.

It was a terrible pity that he did not communicate the same message to the parents.

Stephen was so glad that he was teaching more than a hundred miles from his home in Dublin. If his parents were to hear of this, they would be so disappointed. It was so disheartening. What could he do but put a brave face on it and carry on?

The final bell of the day marked an end to that day's misery. He would try to keep the best side out. Perhaps, the negative experience could yet become a positive as he moved forward in his career. That was a matter for another day. Right now, he joined several colleagues, who adjourned to the nearby hotel to revive sagging spirits. Such meetings had become purely routine for Jimmy Corrigan, who was immune to any further criticism. He was holding court in the front bar of the *Castlehome Arms*.

'The apple never falls far from the tree. When you meet the parents, you see where the youngsters get their bad manners', he affirmed.
Jimmy was once again on one of his hobbyhorses.
'Just because they went to school themselves, they feel they're all education experts.'
Miss Hayes, the Religious Education teacher, had experienced a quiet day. Those parents who came to speak with her had arrived at her desk late in the day. Their priority was seeing those teaching examination subjects first.
She sat alone for long periods, either gazing vacantly into the distance or writing furiously in her classroom journal. Whenever Simon Lynch came close to her on one of his frequent laps of the room, he lingered for a few moments. Miss Hayes, probably alone of all the staff, seemed to enjoy the principal's conversations and his company.
Stephen imagined that Simon Lynch was ill at ease speaking to Miss Hayes. He was constantly buzzing around her, yet not settling to chat with her. Stephen imagined that he was fearful of being branded a loser for being dependent on the likes of Ellen Hayes for casual conversation. They looked like an unlikely couple as they chatted, the twin pillars of decency and propriety in the school.
When Stephen Daly went to the bar again, he saw that his colleague, Pamela, was at the counter.
'Allow me to get these, Pamela', he chivalrously offered.
'No, thank you, I'm getting a round in', she curtly replied.
The atmosphere between them had taken on a distinctive chill.
Unfazed, he continued in his efforts to be sociable.

'How did the parents' anniversary go? With all that has been happening, I hadn't a chance to see you since. Did they enjoy the occasion?

She responded with forced civility.

'They surely did, thank you. And I hear you had an interesting weekend too.'

The already cool temperature in the air suddenly took a nosedive. Stephen had been caught off-guard by the intensity of the cold war being waged against him. He hated being unpopular and was disappointed that Pamela felt as she did. Nevertheless, he attempted to behave as normally as he possibly could.

'Well, I had a pretty good weekend. I'm sure Sinead told you about the quiz. Did you hear that we got into the prize money?'

The contemptuous manner in which she curled her nose up at this indicated that such matters were of no interest to her.

'Sinead also tells me you are taking her to the pictures tonight', she added scornfully. 'I wouldn't have thought that you were interested in the films', she scoffed.

Stephen was sorry for saying anything beyond a quick greeting. He was determined not to get involved in a slanging match. Pamela was a charming girl who was hurting.

She was attracted to Stephen and naturally felt slighted when he invited her housemate on a date.

'I watch the odd film, he claimed.

Then in an attempt to jolly her along, he adopted a more casual approach.

'Didn't we watch a good film together last week?'

'As I recall, you slept right through that entire film', she retorted, delighted with a point-scoring opportunity.

She couldn't resist asking him a question.

'*Sleeping with the Enemy*, do you plan to sleep with Sinead tonight?'

To diffuse the situation, Stephen tried to change the subject.

'Did you see many parents today?'

She answered his question, but it was with cold civility. It was clear that her sharp claws were still out. She could not resist another scratch at Stephen.

'I did. It was very tiresome. At least I can get an early night. I'm not likely to be going out socialising, unlike other people I know'.

This situation was getting increasingly uncomfortable for Stephen. Nevertheless, for some unknown reason, he kept up the conversation. Perhaps he felt it might be better to allow her an opportunity to let off steam.

'Sinead mentioned that you and Susan are not really into films'.

'She was right. I prefer to live in the real world. I don't need to go in for that kind of escapism'.

Talking of escapism reminded Stephen that he still had two working legs under him.

He muttered something about catching up with her later. There was no further response from Pamela. She had said all that she wished to say. After lifting her tray of drinks from the counter, she retreated to the back of the bar room.

Left alone, Stephen took a deep breath and wondered how he could have played it any differently. He hated to have an atmosphere between them. Pam was a genuinely nice girl. However, there was no chemistry between them, from his side anyway. Pamela simply did not light his fire. There was no point in worrying about it now. He had to go home and change to be ready to pick Sinead up at eight.

When Stephen Daly called to pick up Sinead, it was Pamela who answered the door. That was the worst of those girls living together. Still, he just had to accept it as the new reality.
Pamela's mood had not improved in the interim, and she was as sarcastic as ever.
'Well, if it's not our little film buff, Stephen Daly. And what may I ask is your recommendation for tonight?' she sarcastically asked.
Sinead fetched her coat and made her way to the door. Stephen had feared that Sinead might well cancel their arrangement in the light of all that transpired, but he felt encouraged that she had not done so.
'Try not to make too much noise when you come home, Sinead. Remember, I'm a very light sleeper'.
Once out of earshot, Stephen asked.
'What's wrong with her?'
He asked as if he did not already know the answer to that question.
He was interested to know Sinead's angle on the whole business.
'I don't think that she approves of me going out with you, Stephen', she replied in a surprisingly matter-of-fact tone.
'What's wrong with me? He asked with an air of injured innocence.
'I'm not some sort of psycho or stalker', he said shamelessly, fishing for any compliment that might come his way
'I should certainly hope not', she said, settling her hair outside of her coat.
'Maybe, she had hoped that you might ask her on a date'.
'Sinead, I'm sorry if I did anything to give her that impression. I realise that it can't be easy for you to share a house with her right now.

'You can say that again. I was on the point of cancelling our arrangement this evening. I don't need this hassle. But then I asked myself why I should live my life around someone else's moods?'

As Stephen listened, there was plenty to mull over.
It was apparent that Sinead could take him or leave him. Despite his rising hopes, he had not swept her off her feet. She was also a tough, independent girl who would live her life the way she wanted to live it. However, the whole business was upsetting for both of them. The tedious and annoying shadow of Pamela was hanging over the evening. It was difficult to have romantic thoughts in such an atmosphere. But, like the Bard said: 'Venus smiles not in a house of tears.'
There was already a queue forming at the Odeon, so they took their place under the tattered canopy.

Sinead was dressed in a black mini skirt, which gloriously accentuated her long supermodel legs. Stephen even remarked that it was the first time that he had seen her legs. In the past, Sinead had opted for the more casual attire of jeans.
'Well, what do you think of them?
'I think they suit you down to the ground'.
The inevitable busker made his appearance. He slung his guitar over his shoulder and proceeded to affix a mouth organ to metal supports attached to his guitar. Then, in a voice that was far from melodic, he commenced his rather limited repertoire. The old standards *Raglan Road* and *The Fields of Athenry* were cruelly savaged and reduced to pale shadows of their original forms.

For whatever reason, the opening of the cinema doors had been delayed. This development served to expose the merry balladeer's pathetically limited repertoire. With a fast-moving queue, the patrons would at most hear his rendition of just two ballads. Tonight showed that they were missing nothing. He was like a gramophone with a broken needle, spewing out mind-numbing repetition. Eventually, the doors opened. The waiting patrons filed in, relieved at their escape from the dubious entertainer.

After a few minutes in the darkened cinema, Stephen wondered whether he should be doing something. He understood that a faint heart never won a fair lady. However, he did not know what might be expected of him. He often saw the leading man in a film place his hand on the girl's knee and still not have it amputated. He decided to take a chance.

However, that approach was unwelcome. Sinead grabbed his hand and replaced it gently but firmly on the armrest.

'Do you have Italian relations?'

'No, why do you ask?'

'It's just that you have Roman hands. At least, they were roaming all over my leg'.

At least that remark showed that she was not angry about it

'You should get that hand checked out. It seems to have a mind of its own'.

She smiled but was not welcoming the return of the roman hands.

Having turned to concentrate on the screen for a few moments,

Stephen became aware of some commotion behind him. It quickly registered with him that he was the target of the remarks.
The utterances were frequent and timed to coincide with the audience reaction to what was happening on screen.
'Daly, you big wanker you!'
'Go back to Dublin, you useless fucker'.
'You can't fucking teach for nuts'.

Stephen was seething with anger. He chose to ignore them, but it was very embarrassing. He felt that he was at least entitled to live his life without this sort of moronic behaviour. Thankfully it subsided after a few moments. Sinead reached over and touched his hand.
'Don't worry, love. They are not worth getting upset over. You can sort them out at school'.
That was easier said than done.
Those boys were cowardly operating under the cover of darkness. He felt certain that they would have sneaked out of the cinema ahead of him. Things were going from bad to worse. These boys neither feared nor respected him. It was so unfair and inappropriate that he was being targeted in his private life. This was not good enough. Sinead advised him to ignore them and not give them the attention they craved. He did as she asked. Still, he knew that people like that do not stop until they are confronted. However, this was not the occasion to engage with them.

Understandably, Stephen was feeling angry and humiliated. Sinead wanted to take his mind off the incident, so she suggested that they go for a Chinese meal. The business was brisk at the Chinese restaurant. There was a ten-minute wait for a table. Having ordered some drinks, they waited in the anteroom until a table became available.

Sinead retired to the lady's room. On her way back, she fell into conversation with a nursing colleague, who had also been to the cinema. Stephen reddened as he saw them chat and then look in his direction. He dreaded to think what they might be saying. He hoped that Sinead had not mentioned how he had been on the receiving end of verbal abuse from some unmannerly kids. He wasn't to know that Sinead's nursing colleague had witnessed the whole thing.

To pass the time, he put down his head and took to playing with his mobile phone. Finally, he raised his head on hearing his name being called in soft, dulcet tones. He was shocked to find Eva Lynch standing over him.

Stephen again felt himself becoming breathless and flustered. Once again, she had approached him unseen. The fact that she was standing while he was sitting put him at a greater disadvantage. He followed his instinct and stood up.

'What brings you here?' he instinctively asked. As soon as he had uttered the words, he knew how ridiculous the question had been. After all, Eva was not in a Chinese takeaway to have a manicure.

'Getting a takeaway for my supper. I've had a long day. I'm just back from Dublin. I'm feeling peckish.'

After a long day, she looked as if she had just stepped out of a boutique window. Dressed in her finely tailored business suit, she wore tinted driving glasses, which she had pushed back on her head.

'What do you work at?' He asked the question as much to keep talking as to elicit information.
'I work with the Hibernia Building Society. I visit branches in the Western region, liaising with branch managers to ensure everything is in order. Then, I report, what I have learned, to our head office in Dublin'.
'That would certainly keep you pretty busy then'.
'Yea, it keeps me out of trouble'.
She looked at his phone on the table.
'I like that phone. Is that a recent model?'
'Yea, it is. I got an upgrade a couple of weeks ago'.
She complained about her phone and explained that her employer provided the phone.
'It is not very stylish, and today it was not very useful either. The network was down for several hours, so that was not great service at all. It came back although it's still a bit slow'.
Stephen was mesmerised by the woman, but he was anxious not to appear distracted. He was desperately trying to look composed, but his efforts were in vain.
'The service here is a bit slow for a Wednesday night, I suppose.'
Eva smiled sweetly.
'I was talking about the phone service.'

Stephen blushed with embarrassment. He again felt juvenile and foolish in her presence. Eva was an experienced woman of the world who could read a man very well. She could see that she had an unsettling influence on Stephen, and she was pleased with that. What

Stephen Daly could not have guessed was that he had a mesmerising effect upon her as well.

'Can I take a closer look at your phone?'

Stephen readily agreed.

Eva took the phone in her hand and examined its size and lightweight feel. She even scrolled through some of the phone's settings. For a moment, he thought that Eva might be making a call. He certainly hoped that she was not calling her husband's number from his device. That would be so awkward.

Stephen checked to see if Sinead was returning to him.

As Eva returned his phone, Stephen had the unnerving sensation that this woman could read his thoughts. She seemed not alone able to recognise his discomfort but to revel in it.

'Are you waiting for a takeaway yourself?'

He informed her that he was waiting for a table.

'There seems to be a big crowd sitting down in there tonight'.

'Oh, out with the girlfriend, is it?'

'No, it's just a friend. Sinead is a good friend. We were at the pictures together.'

It would have been easier just to answer 'Yes, she is my girlfriend'. After all, that is what he hoped Sinead would be after tonight. But, for some reason, he didn't tell the truth. The older woman always seemed to unnerve him.

'Doing anything special for the Halloween break?' she asked.

'The family is taking off to the sun, so I am house-sitting for a while'.

With that, Sinead returned from her chat and was shyly introduced to Eva.
'Would you care to join us in a quick drink while you are waiting?' Stephen asked.
'No thanks, but maybe another night,' she added suggestively.'
'I think that I'll hit straight home. I could go to bed this very minute. But some other night, Stephen', she repeated.

Eva's order was ready to be collected. As she moved to the till, Sinead had a good look at her.
'That woman was a bit overfriendly for my liking.'
He explained who she was. Sinead paid her what Stephen considered to be a questionable compliment.
'She's an elegant looking older lady. I hope I look as well when I'm her age.'
Stephen was a bit surprised that Eva Lynch would be dismissed as some older woman.
'She's not old, Sinead. It's just that she's not young. She's not in her twenties like we are.'
Sinead was not for budging on that issue.
'She is not, and she's not in her thirties either. So, I would say that she is fairly tearing through her forties pretty rapidly'.
Stephen decided that it might be better to drop the subject.
'Come on; we should place our order now. It will speed things up for when we get a table'.
Sinead opted for the *Sweet 'N' Sour Chicken.* Stephen did likewise. He also ordered a bottle of the House White to accompany the food.

After a few moments, a waitress escorted them to their table in the large dining room. Stephen had been proved right about ordering early. A waitress promptly brought their food. Stephen had begun to put the bad experience of the cinema behind him. Being out with Sinead had been a wonderful distraction. And what was he to make of the attention bestowed on him by Eva Lynch? He knew that he would mull that over when he got home, but Sinead commanded his full attention for the moment.

The conversation was easy and relaxed.

Stephen, who was reluctant to break the evening's magic by a hasty departure, called for a second bottle of wine.

Sinead was clearly at ease also.

'I really enjoyed tonight, Stephen. I hope you did too.'

'I didn't realise that it was over yet. You know lots of things could happen before morning.'

'It will have to be over soon. I have an early start in the morning'.

'I would not mind a twelve-hour shift with you'.

'I know the kind of shift you have in mind, Stephen Daly. Come on, let's get out of here before the alcohol softens your brain completely'.

Stephen asked the restaurant manager to order a taxi

For a change, a car arrived in only a matter of minutes. Wednesday nights would not be too busy for them.

The lights were all off at Sinead's house when they returned. Stephen bravely invited himself in for a cup of coffee. Sinead recommended drinking some water instead after consuming so much alcohol.

'Coffee will only keep you awake'.

'Fine then, it's water for me, if that's what the nurse ordered. And by the way, I think a lie down would do me some good'.

'It certainly would', she answered.

Stephen eased himself onto the sofa and stretched out on it. He took her hand and drew her on top of him.

'You know well that I meant lying down alone in your own bed', she insisted.

'That would do no good,' he lamented. OK then, give me a kiss before I go home'.

Stephen would have been happy with a quick peck on the cheek, followed by a shoe out the door. However, he was delighted when she threw her arms around his neck, drew him to her and gave him a long passionate kiss.

He thought that he might faint from pure bliss.

On his walk home, despite his humiliation in the cinema, Stephen felt a warm, satisfied glow inside of him. He considered that the evening had worked out well for him. The thought of school the next morning soon lessened that glow.

Bangers and stink bombs were the perennial scourge in the week leading up to Halloween. Stephen's classroom had been a target of the phantom bombers on two different occasions, thus adding to his increasing longing for the midterm break.
It was a particularly wet morning. Tom's car was in the garage for some minor repairs, resulting from a difference of opinion with a lamppost. Having walked to school, Tom was drenched to the skin, as was Stephen, who had accompanied him through the downpour. With twenty minutes to spare, they were both standing in the empty staff room, their clothes dripping water.

Tom proceeded to remove his rain-soaked trousers in typically uninhibited style before draping them over one of the radiators in the room. Another radiator was commandeered to hold his wet shirt and socks. Stephen, always a much more self-conscious soul, opted to remain in his wet clothes.
As the steam was rising from the drenched garments, the performer in Tom broke through. Grabbing a broom handle from the corner of the room, he jumped up on the table. In his semi-nude state, he gave what he imagined to be a stage performance to rival Elvis Presley at his best.
♫ *You ain't nothing- but a hound - dog*! ♫

Stephen imagined that there would be some fun should Miss Hayes walk into the room at that moment.
'She would have a stroke', Stephen reckoned.
'No, I don't think she'd be quick enough.' Tom laughed.

'You have a one-track mind, Tom. And by the way, those Man. United Y fronts aren't exactly in keeping with the Elvis image. Maybe a pair of blue suede ones might be better; to match the shoes".

'Suede drawers! What do you take me for? Get lost Daly,' replied Tom as he launched into another love song from The King.

♫*I guess -I'll never -know the-reason -why"*
You love me as -you do,
Yes- that's the the-wonder---♫

Unlike Tom, Stephen could hear footsteps approaching. Uncharitably, he chose not to alert Tom, but rather shouted encouragement to his friend to raise the roof to a crescendo. Tom innocently obliged.

♫*Yes, that's the –wonder- the wonder-of you-----youuuuuuuu*♫

Lynch, on arrival in the room, stared incredulously at Tom. His mouth hung open. The principal seemed momentarily lost for words. This was a new one for him. When Tom became aware of his principal's presence, he almost fell off the table. He was both startled and mortally embarrassed. He cut a most pathetic figure with his bare white chest, dressed only in his teenage style underwear, perched on the staff room table, still gripping the old broom handle. His tomato-red face was looking down on the now purple-faced principal.

'The lunatics have taken over the asylum. Mr Clarke, you are to get down at once, get dressed and meet me in my office in five minutes. And you had better have a good explanation for this utterly unprofessional and outrageous behaviour.'

After Lynch departed, a much-deflated Tom descended from the table with an incredulous look on his face.

'How in the hell did that gobshite get in without either of us hearing him?'

Stephen had not the heart to confess that indeed he had heard him approach. He was feeling more than a little guilty about getting his friend into trouble but still not so sorry as would prevent him from having a damn good laugh at his expense.

'The singing must have drowned out the sound', he lamely suggested.

Tom was taking his still steaming clothes from the radiator and getting dressed to meet Lynch.

'Stephen, there was a second there, and I don't mind admitting it when I thought I was going to shit in my shorts. He scared the living daylights out of me. Now he'll probably make mincemeat of me altogether when I go to the office'.

Stephen tried to be comforting.

'Listen to me. Unlike me, you have a permanent contract. Simon Lynch couldn't dislodge you now, not even with a crowbar. Anyway, it's not a hanging offence unless-!

'Unless what?'

"Unless he's a Liverpool supporter."

'Give me a break, Daly'.

Tom left the staff room and headed off to face the real music, the steam still rising from his half-dried clothes.

On the day that school finished for the midterm, Stephen gratefully accepted a lift to Dublin from Jimmy Corrigan. Jimmy was visiting an elderly uncle in hospital and was glad of some company. Stephen was delighted with the offer. It meant that he would have a couple of more hours with his family before they headed off to sunnier climes.

Stephen soon discovered that Jimmy was a very impatient and erratic driver. He tended to shout and angrily gesticulate at other road users. His tolerance threshold was equally low inside and outside the classroom. The conversation on the way up had very little got to do with school.

Stephen talked of the week ahead and the plans he had. His parents were going to Gran Canaria for two weeks, accompanied by his two younger sisters, Niamh, aged seventeen and Lorraine, aged fifteen. Stephen had opted to stay at home. The plan was that Stephen would drive them to the airport in his father's car. After that, he would have his dad's car for the fortnight. His father had generously insured him on the vehicle. As of now, he intended to drive down to Castlehome the next week and take Sinead for a drive on one of her days off.

En route, he filled in Corrigan on the sorry state of his relationship with Pamela. The older man was already aware of the fact that there was a lot of tension between them. But, interestingly, he found his colleague to be surprisingly sympathetic to Pamela's feelings.

'Be nice to that girl. She's probably feeling a bit fragile now'.

He suggested that Stephen contact her over the weekend and offer her a lift back to Castlehome after the break. You are practically going past her door anyway'.
'Whatever issue ye might have won't be sorted out until you can talk it through.'
Even Stephen could see a clear logic to that.
'You could offer her a seat back to Castlehome'.
'Ah, she'd never go for that, Jimmy. She'd probably tell me to get lost. She probably has a return ticket for the train'.
'My advice is that you sort it out before you go back, or you will have it festering for God knows how long.'
Stephen accepted that Corrigan was right about sorting this business out once and for all. Stephen needed more time to think about it, so he decided to sleep on it.
Two hours out, on a stretch of road, which was under repair, an impatient Corrigan found himself behind two slow-moving articulated lorries. There was little or no space to overtake. Whenever the road was wide enough to pass, there was invariably an untimely procession of cars coming from the opposite direction.

He seemed determined to overtake before he reached the next bend in the road. He didn't want to be tailing them for maybe the next twenty miles. As he completed the manoeuvre, the speedometer was showing sixty. The signposting indicated that there was a thirty miles limit on that stretch of road.
It was too late to slow down when he spotted the Garda checkpoint. Unable to stop on command, he managed to bring the car to a halt

some yards ahead of them. A young garda approached. He did not look too impressed. After watching Corrigan's car screech to a delayed halt, his colleague continued to check the traffic travelling in the opposite direction.

Jimmy Corrigan realised that he was in trouble. He became uncharacteristically flustered and fidgety. This incident could cost him dearly.

'I don't think they had their speed guns out. They probably can't do me for exceeding the speed limit.

Stephen was not too confident on that score.

'Christ Jimmy, they'd know you were doing more than thirty. You weren't even able to stop. They could do you on a reckless driving charge anyway.'

The fresh-faced garda was now level with the car. Corrigan rolled down the window, prepared for the worst. The young officer first circled the car, checking lights, tyres and windscreen discs.

'Let me do the talking.'

Corrigan advised.

'You just keep quiet'.

'I had no intention of talking, Jimmy. You got yourself into this one, so best of luck in getting out of it'.

The garda stuck his head into the car surveying the two nervous occupants. His eyes slowly and deliberately scanned the interior as if he was looking for someone in particular. For a moment, there was a slight hope that maybe this checkpoint was part of a search for a known criminal.

'Well, where is she?' he asked, eyes wide open with feigned wonder.

'Where is who? Who is it that you are looking for, Sergeant?' Jimmy asked, hoping that he might win him over with a dollop of flattery.

'The woman in labour! I was certain that you were rushing to the hospital. And it's plain ordinary, Guard, for the moment anyway'.

'Not for long, I predict'.

Jimmy hoped that a little flattery might prove decisive.

Stephen felt sorry for Corrigan. Not only had he been nabbed, but he also had the misfortune to encounter a right smart-ass. Nevertheless, his friend was trying his best to extricate himself from the mess that he had created.

'There is no pregnant woman. My friend here is very sick. I'm rushing to get him home.'

'I see, and what is the nature of his illness?' asked the garda.

Jimmy was wracking his brains for an acute medical condition, consistent with the ability to sit upright, consume alcohol from a can and present with a very red face.

'He's suffering from Irritable Bowel Syndrome.'

The guard realised that he had Jimmy where he wanted him. Like a cat playing with a mouse, he wished to prolong the fun for him and the misery for Jimmy Corrigan

'A man on the run, is it? He said, laughing at his own joke.

Jimmy nodded in agreement.

'I don't think alcohol is a cure for your condition.'

The young garda allowed that issue to rest for a moment.

His next issue was the absence of an insurance disc.

'It is insured all right, as I'm sure you'll find out, but one of the children must have pulled it down. I swear to you that it is insured'.
The officer of the law summed up the situation.
'You have been observed driving over the maximum speed limit on a dangerous stretch of road. Furthermore, you are driving a car with two tyres below the legal minimum thread depth. As well as that, you have no current insurance disc displayed. Therefore, I must inform you that you are liable to be prosecuted under the *Road Traffic Act 1961'.*
'The thing is,' interrupted Corrigan. 'I'm thinking of trading the car in and getting another in Dublin. This man is a mechanic. He's going to check out some of the cars for me'.
The young policeman nodded.
'If his condition improves, I suppose'.
With every word he spoke, Stephen hated this young man more. He felt sure that this sarcasm was reserved for the relatively innocent lawbreakers. He could not imagine him behaving similarly with subversives or other potentially violent criminals.

It registered with Stephen that the young garda may have suspected that Jimmy Corrigan had been drinking. However, this was not the case as Jimmy was in school all morning.
'Would you mind stepping out of the car, Sir and open up your boot for me, please?'
Jimmy successfully passed this part of the test. The young garda glanced into the open boot.
The law enforcement officer smirked and shook his head.

'Not alone is your spare tyre as flat as a pancake. It is as bald as your two front tyres'.

The second officer approached to see what was happening. He looked some years older than his colleague. They say that the devil's children have the devil's luck. That was true for Jimmy Corrigan, on this occasion anyway. It transpired that the older garda was a past pupil of Jimmy Corrigan.

'Jaysus, if it's not Mr Corrigan. How are you anyway?

'Call me, Jimmy. You are a long way from school now.'

'I remember well you trying to teach us all those silly theorems in Maths, for all the good they ever did us. Fancy seeing you again! Are you still in St. Jude's?

Jimmy looked as relieved as any man whose death sentence had been commuted.

'I am still there. They can't get rid of me now, Joseph, isn't it? Oh yea, I remember your class all right. That must be over fifteen years ago'.

'It is and more. It is eighteen years,' replied Joseph, suitably amazed at the rapid passage of time.

'Well, Joseph, this here is Stephen Daly. He's an English teacher at the college. He just started in September'.

'Not a mechanic then?' interrupted the first garda, scratching his chin and looking rather puzzled.

Stephen and Jimmy chose to ignore the remark.

'Jimmy, tell me this, did you ever marry?'

To students, Jimmy was always presumed to be a bachelor.

'Well, I did marry. However, it didn't work out. The only good thing was that there were no kids, so the damage was limited'.
The younger garda seemed to have softened his approach and was warming to the newfound civility.
'You are probably better off without children anyway. They would only be ripping down the insurance disc from your windscreen'.
Once again, his contribution passed unnoticed.
'I'm in the force ten years now. I've just recently passed for sergeant'.
'Well done, man, congratulations, you're fairly moving up the ladder', uttered a suitably impressed Corrigan.
Garda Joseph shyly but proudly accepted his former teacher's congratulations.

Joseph and Jimmy spent some minutes reminiscing about the college of yesteryear. They especially recalled soccer successes. The conversation over, Jimmy took his leave, without any further reference by either garda to Corrigan's alleged motoring offences. Jimmy heaved one massive sigh of relief. He had been saved an awful lot of bother and expense.
Sometimes, it was clearly an advantage at times to be a St. Jude's teacher.
'Christ, I got out of jail there, but that was too close for comfort'.
There was no arguing with that.
'How do you feel when you meet former students?' Stephen asked.

Jimmy had no problem with such encounters.
'It's generally no problem at all. Still, I have to laugh at the way they always ask if you are still teaching. What do they expect? Do they

think that I might have changed jobs and gone flipping burgers in *Mc Donalds*?'

It had been a random remark by the older man. However, he did not know that his younger colleague had given very serious consideration to that very move.

Stephen was intrigued to see the rapport, which existed between Corrigan and his former student. The garda officer clearly held Jimmy in affection. It had been great to witness.

'I don't know if that will happen for me', said Stephen. 'I'm not sure I'm cut out for this lark. Don't get me wrong. I like the actual teaching. If only I were allowed to teach. Sometimes I think my whole world is collapsing in on me.'

Corrigan provided a sympathetic ear and actually made some very astute observations.

'I can sympathise with it. The way it is, Stephen, it's more and more becoming a case of teaching students who do not want to learn. My simple advice to you, for what it is worth, is that you should give St. Jude's until the end of the year and then get to hell out of the place, and start afresh somewhere new'.

There was merit in that advice from Jimmy. Stephen looked at him but did not reply as the older colleague had more to say on the matter.

'And don't forget that you are a total, raw recruit this year. I still have nightmares about my first year of teaching. I had no control at all. My classes did not take a blind bit of notice of me. They were even jumping in and out of the windows. I gave it one year and then moved on. When I got my second job, I had learned from my mistakes. None of us is born competent. It's a skill that you have to develop, not that I ever became a shining example of a good teacher', he confessed.

Stephen stubbornly clung to the hope that things would get better for him in St. Jude's. Hadn't Tom told him that it was easier after the first year?

But, in his heart of hearts, he knew that he would need to be rid of much of the current cohort of students and then make a more determined effort with the incoming students.

As Sinead had a day off on Monday, Stephen travelled to Castlehome to take her on a day trip to Galway. He was looking forward to the trip and having a monopoly on her time for some hours anyway. He was feeling better now that he was on a break from school. It was the first Monday morning in months that he did not wake with a feeling of anxiety.

He appreciated his father generosity in allowing him to drive his car. It had been great to catch up with his mum and dad. But now he had other things on his mind. Stephen Daly was more than happy at the way the relationship with Sinead was progressing. He felt more and more at ease with her and could be his natural and true self. There seemed less need to impress her now.

Like most teachers, he knew his timetable by heart. Each class represented a different variety of misery. Whenever he was on a break from school, he appreciated the freedom.

Sinead was not impressed.

'I never met such clock watchers as teachers.'

'How would they feel if they had to do twelve-hour shifts and be ran off their feet from eight till eight.'

'Being busy is not a problem', Stephen stated.

'I'd love to be so busy that the time would fly. If a patient is doing a urine test, you don't have to coach them for it. Nobody would view you as a failure if the patient doesn't take his medicine at home. You don't have to take hospital work home with you. And you never have patients cat calling you in the cinema'.

Sinead could see that this was more than just grumbling about a job. It was almost a cry of despair.
'That was awful in the cinema. It gave me a good insight into what you have to deal with'.
'Are you sure the job is worth all the stress that it is causing you, Stephen?'
He had been thinking the same thing himself.
'I think you could be right. I have no problem being a teacher, but I wasn't trained to be a jail warden or policeman or even a bouncer.'
Sinead reached across and lightly touched his cheek.
'Come on, Stephen, that is a talk for another day. It's a day off. Forget the job. Let's just make the most of our free day together'.
On the way to Galway, Sinead told him that there was a very bad atmosphere in her house. Pamela had convinced herself that only for Sinead's manoeuvrings that Stephen would have dated her. The notion was absurd, yet that feeling had driven a wedge between them. She predicted that Pamela would have something to say when she heard about this day trip. Stephen did not want anything to distract from the wonderful atmosphere of this day.
'You can't live your life based on what someone else might think'.
'I know you are right. OK then, I understand that school and Pamela Mc Enroe are two subjects banned for the remainder of the day'.

Even though it was late October, it was a bright and sunny day in the Western capital. The sun was generously casting its warming rays on the mid-morning streets, enticing the early risers to shed the outer layers of their seasonal attire. Of course, the afternoon crowds would soon pack these quiet and winding streets on this glorious autumn day. However, for now, the young couple were free to enjoy the old city in relative peace.

Sinead was interested in buying some clothes. Stephen proposed that they split up for an hour and a half and meet up for something to eat. He enjoyed a walk around town and sat down for a coffee and a read of the newspaper.

Sinead took her time in the shops and came back laden down with purchases. She even bought a new casual jacket for him as well as a chunky fisherman's pullover. He had reservations about whether this suited him or not. Sinead joked that he should ignore his opinion, as she was the arbiter of good taste.

They drove the few miles to Salthill in the afternoon, where they walked the beach before heading out the Barna road. A frosty chill was beginning to creep into the evening. Sinead snuggled close to Stephen as the dark clouds closed in. It had been a delightful day. Both seemed anxious to cling to its treasured remnants.

As it transpired, that day trip was the only outing that he and Sinead enjoyed over the mid-term break. Sinead's grandfather died suddenly, so she had to be out of town for several days. As there was now nothing to keep him, he returned to Dublin, spending the remaining days in the capital. He missed his family but was delighted that they were enjoying their sun holiday. It was time that the dark clouds broke for them too. As Stephen looked back on that trip to Galway, he recalled, with pleasure, many aspects of the day. He and Sinead had been drawn closer together. Both felt comfortable confiding in the other. A problem shared was a load lightened. In bed that night, he thanked God for sending such a wonderful girl into his life.

Corrigan's suggestion about offering Pamela a lift back to Castlehome on Sunday evening held some merit for Stephen. He desperately wanted to clear the air with her. From a purely selfish viewpoint alone, life would be less complicated if they talked again. Pamela was just hurting.

While the staff room in St. Jude's might be big enough to avoid each other, the fact that Pamela lived with Sinead complicated matters. Nevertheless, he vowed that he was going to make the call and do as Jimmy had advised.

Directory Enquiries came up with a number for her parents' home in Mullingar. Her mother answered the telephone. As luck would have it, Pamela was out, but her mother was only too delighted to arrange a lift on her daughter's behalf.

She told him that Pamela hated travelling on the train on Sunday evenings. There were seldom any free seats by the time it reached Mullingar. Pam's mum seemed a pleasant, chatty lady who spoke quite like her daughter.

It had been a stroke of luck that Pamela was not at home. She would have almost certainly have spurned his offer. She might still attempt to frustrate it, but Stephen was alert to that possibility. When Mrs Mc Enroe asked for his phone number to enable Pamela to confirm the arrangement, he evaded the question. He felt quite sure that Pamela would ring him to put an end to any such idea. Stephen assured Mrs

Mc Enroe that Mullingar was on his route. Even if he had to go a few miles off the bypass, it meant nothing to him.
After getting the necessary directions, Stephen pondered his next move. One thing was abundantly clear. Pamela had mentioned nothing to them about any problems with Stephen. Therefore, it was unlikely that she would now wish to paint that particular picture for them.

The following morning Stephen was unsure about the situation with Pamela. He had been half-expecting a call from her to cancel the arrangement.
Just as he was stepping out of the shower, his mobile phone rang. The caller's voice was soft and feminine and had a now-familiar timbre. The caller immediately identified herself simply as Eva. Even though she was miles away from him, he felt his pulse rate quicken.
'Stephen, love, I hope that I'm not disturbing you too early in the morning. Are you still in Dublin?'
He assured her that he was speaking to her from Dublin.
If only she had known that he was speaking to her in a state of total undress.
'Stephen, I'm up in Dublin for a meeting and staying the night in a dreadfully boring old hotel. I normally dine with an old school friend of mine. The trouble is that she is out of town this evening. If you are at a loose end, might you ever do me a huge favour and keep me company?'
Stephen was momentarily lost for words.
As there was no immediate response, Eva continued talking. It was clear to her that she was not pushing an open door. She had to work harder to convince the young man.
'I dread the prospect of dining alone. You can imagine the unwelcome attention I would attract'.
He did not know what to say. Once again, his mind advised one thing while his body advised something else.

Eva was not expecting such a slow response and was surprised at the delay.
'It won't take much more than an hour. Everything would go on the expense account. You would be wined and dined like royalty. The best thing is that it wouldn't cost you a penny. Come on, Stephen, don't deny a damsel in distress.'
Stephen was slowly regaining the use of his vocal cords. At least she was too far away to hear the pounding of his excited heart.

He didn't invite the feelings that he was experiencing, nor could he understand them. Eva Lynch had not featured in his thoughts since their rather embarrassing first meeting. He mustered up sufficient breath to give a qualified acceptance of her invitation even though he wanted to decline politely. Deep down, he felt that he might well regret the decision.
'I will join you for dinner. However, I don't think it is advisable. After all, you are my principal's wife'.
'I would like to think that you could see me as a woman in my own right'.
'I do see you as a woman in your own right. However, I can't help thinking that you are also married to a man who could scupper my professional career.'
'I guarantee you that Simon will know nothing about this, not that he would be too bothered. We have been living separate lives for years'.
Stephen was not currently inclined to pursue that point.
'By the way, Eva, how did you manage to get my mobile number?'
His question seemed to disappoint her.

'There is no great mystery there. You had your mobile phone on the table when we met in the Chinese restaurant. I just dialled my number from your mobile. You didn't hear the ring because I had it in silent mode since my earlier meetings. You had my number too, should you have felt like ringing me'.

This frank account of her underhand methods flattered and unsettled him. He quickly realised that he was dealing with a determined and capable lady.

It was tantamount to an admission that she was attracted to him and had her strategy worked out. He did not like to see himself as being prey to her predatory instincts. But what was he doing accepting her invitation to dinner? He thought of changing his mind and nipping this in the bud, but something inside of him would not allow him to take this course of action.

She told him that she was spending the day in Dublin dealing with some corporate accounts. She should be out of the office by six o'clock. It would take another hour to update her paperwork.

Stephen arranged to meet her outside the dining room of the hotel for an eight-thirty reservation. She asked him to be punctual, as she hated hanging around hotel bars or lobbies on her own.

'I find that it attracts the wrong sort of attention', she said.

He assured her that he would be punctual.

It was akin to a morbidly obese man being offered his fill of the finest food in a top restaurant. It was ever so tempting and yet potentially deadly for him. Stephen honoured his commitment but was not blind to the consequences. This woman certainly had him enraptured. It was a constant struggle for Stephen Daly to appear composed as he sat across from Eva Lynch in the bustling dining room. In an attempt to preserve perspective, he kept reminding himself that this frighteningly sexy lady opposite him was his principal's wife.

This woman, for whom he was feeling scandalous desire, was old enough to be his mother. Even her twin daughters were closer to his age than she was. After all, this was old Simon Lynch's wife. The fact that he was making progress with Sinead made it all the more ridiculous.

However, her powerful magnetism drew him to her to such an extent that reason had been overruled. Her touch, when it lingered, sent a powerful erotic charge through his excited body. He realised that he was well out of his depth.

Stephen was sweating so profusely that he felt embarrassed. He excused himself before making his way to the toilets, where he ran cold water from the tap over his face and his wrists. When he took a look at himself in the mirror, he saw a very frightened young man looking back at him. The thought of taking flight had crossed his mind. However, as the meal was already in progress, it would be an inconsiderate thing to stand up a lady who had been gracious enough to treat him to a meal. He took a deep breath and tried to compose himself.

Returning to the dining room, he sat down and straightened himself up in the chair. He attempted to banish all thoughts of carnal pleasure from his mind, even trying to imagine that Ellen Hayes was his dining companion. That only worked for a moment or two. He attempted to focus on the food but to little avail. He even tried to imagine his mother viewing this scene. Even that proved ineffective.

Eva looked radiant and had doubtlessly taken time out to dress for dinner. She was dressed in a rather formal full-length black dress with a tantalisingly thigh-high slit. Through a combination of the free-flowing wine and Eva's seductive charms, Stephen gradually became more composed, even relaxed. Soon, he was even able to converse without stumbling over his words. He wondered why this might be the case.

Observing her demeanour, he noted that, unlike him, she appeared totally at ease. Eva was charming, witty and seemed very relaxed.

For the next two hours, they chatted, sipped wine and even permitted prolonged silences to reign without either feeling the need to make conversation.

She filled him in on her employment and lifestyle. Nevertheless, she appeared much more interested in talking about him, especially about his relationship with Sinead.

Stephen gave the impression that Sinead was little more than a good friend. He felt guilty about this but in Eva's company, Sinead, for some reason, seemed to take on less significance.

Two postprandial brandies were called for. Rather than adjourn to the plush but public lobby, Eva suggested retiring to her room.

Stephen's initially declined this invitation. However, Eva proved to be very persuasive. Before he knew it, he was seated self-consciously on the well-sprung bed while Eva calmly sat alongside him, still cupping the brandy glass in her left hand. With the other hand, she traced the top rim of the glass with her slender fingers while stealing furtive glances at her nervous companion. As she moved closer, their thighs touched. Stephen mumbled incoherent and thoughtless judgements on the hotel décor in a vain attempt to appear composed.

It was difficult to keep up the pretence of conducting a normal conversation as the blood riotously charged through his manly veins. Embarrassed, he struggled to contain his excitement. The thought crossed his mind that Eva may have been expecting him to make the first move. She was likely to be disappointed on that front, as Stephen was too nervous to initiate anything more demanding than a conversation.

After what seemed ages, Eva reached out her hand and traced the contours of his face with the same circular motion, which she had practised earlier on the rim of her brandy glass. Gently stroking his cheeks, her fingers settling sensually on his impatient lips. Drawing her closer to him, she pressed her mouth onto his, almost stifling him with a series of deep and hungry kisses. As she did so, she rose to her feet and pulled down the zipper at the back of her dress. She eased the dress from her shoulders, allowing it to fall sensuously from her now exposed shoulders and onto the floor.

It was time to go now, but again, his common sense had been overruled. The sight of this ravishingly beautiful woman, so sensuously disrobing before his very eyes, was already pushing Stephen to the limits of self-control. Never in his wildest dreams did he imagine that he could have been so lucky with any woman, much less one he most desired.

Eva stood totally before him in her naked glory. She looked as if she were waiting for his approval. It was more than Stephen felt able to cope with.

Eva, sensing his nervousness, immediately took charge.

Stephen felt pathetically juvenile in her presence. He feared that his inexperience would be ruinous. Trying in vain to steer his mind to less erotic thoughts, he closed his eyes as Eva pleasured him. Soon, their two naked bodies lay entwined, joyfully pleasuring one another.

Eva skilfully directed the subsequent scenes, which exhausted every ounce of the young man's energy.

Her curvaceous body wrapped itself around him. As he stroked her soft, fragrant hair, he again kissed her softly on the lips. They did not speak, nor did either of them feel the need to do so. They lay side by side in silence until sleep overtook them.

It was the morning after the night before. When Stephen opened his eyes, it took him a few moments to get his bearings. What must surely have been a dream was not a dream after all.

Eva Lynch was first to awake and was already preparing for the day ahead of her. Again, she was standing a few feet away from him, this time fully dressed, in fact impeccably so, in yet another finely tailored business suit. She had showered and changed without disturbing him and was now ready to take on her daily workload. Stephen was still experiencing difficulty in getting his bearings. He was fumbling for his watch to see the exact time.

'You must be a great disappointment to your parents. Is this how you mind the house for them? I hope that they haven't been robbed,' she teased.

His parents' house and its contents were the last things on Stephen's mind at that particular moment.

She drew closer to him.

'Did you enjoy last night?

'Sure did', said Stephen pushing a pillow behind his head as he sat in an upright position.

'I feared that it was all a fantastic dream. Wonderful things like that don't normally happen to me'

'Do you regret what happened?'

She asked with some concern.

'I do not. Maybe, we should have taken some precautions'.

'Like locking the door, is it?'

'No', he replied. 'Like making sure that you don't get.........'

Before he could get the word out, Eva had interrupted him.
'That is not something you or I need to concern ourselves with.'
It was not a point on which he sought clarification.

Eva had to rush to an early morning meeting and had no time for breakfast.
She kissed Stephen goodbye before setting off on her round of meetings. He liked to imagine that they were a happily married couple, waking up to yet another day. He had a day off while she was heading off to work. He wondered did she kiss Simon like that in the mornings. Somehow, he doubted it.
He was immediately sorry that the principal had popped into his head at all. It had done nothing for his mood. He wondered how he could ever look the man in the eye again.

Left alone, Stephen was glad of the time to collect his thoughts. The previous night's events were played and replayed in his mind as he attempted to get a handle on what had happened. He was sure that he would never see Simon Lynch in the same light again. Whether he would ever see his wife in the flesh again was another matter.

On Sunday evening, when he rang the doorbell of the Mc Enroe residence in Mullingar, it was Pamela's mother who answered.
'Hello, you must be Stephen. Pamela is nearly ready. You will have a cup of tea while you wait'.
She rattled that off without seeming to take a second breath.
'There's really no need, Mrs Mc Enroe', he protested.
'I had a cup less than an hour ago.'
Despite his protestations, he was ushered into the living room while she got the tea organised. Pamela's father was already sitting there watching television. Seeing Stephen, he stood up and eyed him before offering his hand for a firm handshake.

While Pamela's mother organised matters in the kitchen, her father engaged Stephen in conversation. Even though it was very friendly and good-humoured, Stephen soon found himself answering a series of questions on his background and interests. It slowly dawned on Stephen that Pamela's dad mistakenly viewed him as her boyfriend.

As Mrs Mc Enroe carried the tray of tea into the room, she good-naturedly interrupted her husband's line of questioning.
'Don't be interrogating our visitor. You know Stephen, once a guard, always a guard.'
As it happened, this particular gentleman was only recently retired from the force.
As Stephen was tucking into a slice of homemade cake, Pamela breezed into the room.
She appeared to be more pleasant than ever.
'Hi, Stephen, thanks for the lift. So tell me, when did you get the car?'

'I didn't. It's my father's car'.

Looking at her father's almost disapproving expression, he quickly added.

'I am insured with a full licence'.

He was keen to reassure them.

Mrs Mc Enroe readily understood why Stephen had volunteered that particular piece of information. Everyone was smiling, even the formerly grumpy Pamela.

Corrigan was right, Stephen decided. He must remember to thank Jimmy when he got back. It was great that the problem had been so easily solved.

In a few minutes, Pamela and Stephen were sitting into the car, which was faced for Castlehome. Pamela's mother sprinkled copious amounts of holy water on them and on the vehicle in order to keep them safe on the road.

'It's OK. I am a careful driver'. Stephen explained.

'You may be a good driver, but what about the motorist that you are meeting?'

She had a point there. Stephen was feeling quite relaxed as Pamela seemed to be in good form. However, before they had travelled five hundred metres down the road, her mood suddenly changed.

She once again donned the face of the scorned woman. She was back on the warpath.

'How dare you embarrass me like that, back there! How dare you come into my parents' house without my permission! How dare you!'

She was becoming alarmingly agitated.

Stephen was dumbfounded. He couldn't believe the transformation. He had been lulled into a false sense of security by the sham display of normality in her parents' house.

Pamela was seething with anger, which she had kept a lid on over the last couple of days.

'What do you think my parents are going to think?'

Stephen, confused by this onslaught, was at a loss for words. Pamela repeated the question twice more with an increasing level of ferocity. He had little choice but to make some sort of response.

'How am I supposed to know how or what they think? They're your parents, after all. You tell me.'

She began, practically spitting fire as she spoke.

'Right then, I'll tell you. My mother and father most likely think that you're my boyfriend. They think that we have been going out together and that I never even told them, not even when you were likely to drop in on them.'

'So, where's the problem?'

'The problem is that we are not going out together. You are not my boyfriend. I am not your girlfriend. For God's sake, you are not even my friend.'

Stephen attempted to be as reasonable as possible.

'Well, I'm sorry to hear that you do not see me as your friend because I like to see you as my friend'.

Pamela seemed almost too upset to articulate her feelings in any coherent form. Instead, she retreated into a silent sulk. Stephen took

advantage of this lull to place on record his innocent motivation. He called to offer her a lift. It was hardly a hanging offence.
She leaned down towards the car radio, turned in up to full volume and sulkily sat bolt upright in the seat, arms folded in front of her. Not another word passed between them for the next half-hour. On one occasion, Stephen dared to lower the radio volume, but Pamela instantly restored its former ear-assailing level.
Some forty miles on, Stephen stopped for petrol at a self-service station. He filled the tank and proceeded to pay in the forecourt shop. Then, returning with an apple and bar of chocolate, he tossed them into her lap.
Pamela had not anticipated such generosity. His generous gesture had wrong-footed her. Yet, she preferred to maintain the obstinate front.
'I don't like plain chocolate.'
Stephen looked at her, unable to credit that this girl could be so childish.
He bitterly regretted having called for her at all. He didn't need this hassle.
Out of total exasperation, he snapped back at her.
'Don't like plain chocolate bars, do you not? I should have known that it would be fruit and nut for you!' he fumed before slapping the car into gear and speeding off down the road to Castlehome.

Total silence continued in the car for about fifteen more seconds before Pamela inexplicably burst out laughing. The exasperated comment acted as a sort of release mechanism to free her from the seething anger. Stephen was at a loss as to what to say. The more she observed this confused expression, the more uncontrollably she laughed. Finally, she composed herself sufficiently to explain her amazing outburst.

'Oh, Stephen Daly, you have the patience of Job to put up with me and my erratic behaviour.'

It took Stephen a further moment or two to realise that this most recent mood change was not just another phase in her onslaught on him. When he was sure that she had called an end to current hostilities, he was only too glad to be gracious. Still, he harboured doubts about the longevity of this transformation.

'I'm sorry. Thank you for the lift. I hate the bloody train. I do appreciate the fact that you thought of me'.

'But why did you kick up such a fuss about it, back the road there?'

'I suppose it was because I am silly and immature. I felt that you were only obliging me out of a sense of duty or worse still charity.'

'And how on earth could you think that?' he asked with a look of pained puzzlement in his weary eyes.

'Don't ask. I'm not even able to explain it to myself.'

The tension that had plagued the car had by now been completely dissipated. She offered her best attempt at explaining her hostile reaction

'Stephen, you know that I like you. I have to confess that I thought that we might get together and I suppose I was disappointed when you dated Sinead'.

Pamela further enquired, if by any chance Sinead had been the one to prompt his offer of the lift from Mullingar.

'No, definitely not! Sinead knows nothing about it. I never told her what my plans were. Anyway, she hasn't been around for a few days. Her grandfather died, so she had to go away to the funeral and took a couple of days of holiday leave as well. She is not due back until tomorrow evening'.

Pamela was quietly pleased to learn that Sinead was in the dark about this. Whatever about calling off hostilities with Stephen, she had no notion of advancing detente with Sinead. On the contrary, she would continue to stir up the division between them. The enforced absence of contact between Sinead and Stephen was welcome news to her. Hope springs eternal in the human breast.

The final miles of the journey passed quite civilly. They engaged in normal conversation about recent happenings in St. Jude's.

When they finally reached Pamela's house, she insisted on his coming in for a cup of coffee. The cup of coffee became two cups before he insisted on crossing the estate to his own house.

For her part, Pamela eagerly awaited her housemate's return.

As sure as night follows day, school re-opening was to be followed by increased levels of stress. On this occasion, Stephen's problems were not confined to the classroom. When he met Sinead on Tuesday evening, he received a very cool reception.
She was livid that Stephen had gone out of his way to bring Pamela back on Sunday evening. If he had told her in advance, it would have been unpleasant, but hearing it second hand from her gloating housemate was doubly upsetting.
It appeared that Pamela had painted a very self-serving account of her trip back to town with Stephen Daly.

She spoke of Stephen telephoning her home in Mullingar and insisting that she travel back with him. She described the cosy scene as he sampled her home baking. She casually mentioned that he had bought her chocolate. There was particular emphasis on their late-night chat in front of the sinking fire. All of this was true but what was false was any insinuation that there had been something approaching intimacy between them.
Stephen could not deny any of this. Nor would he wish to do so. He would have done it all over again, with the probable exception of the chat in her house. Again, he was left floundering in his desperate attempts to understand why Pamela would cause trouble like this when she had seemed to come to peace with the arrangement.
He tried his best to explain everything to Sinead and afterwards felt that Sinead had accepted his version of events.
Stephen had been innocent and naive in supplying ammunition to Pamela in the cold war that continued to rage between the girls.

Stephen felt that destiny must have decreed that he be out of favour with either Sinead or Pamela at any one time. He considered that maybe it was a form of perverted justice for him. He was being reprimanded for being intimate with a woman whom he never touched. At the same time, he had been intimate with a married woman but was getting no grief over that.

He was not the only one with a long face on his return to Saint Jude's College. His mate Tom was not exactly full of the joys of living either. All that Stephen could elicit was that he failed to capture the affections of some girl on whom he had his heart set. Normally Tom's relationships were an open book, on display for all to read. At any rate, Stephen was not particularly bothered. He had more than enough woman trouble himself.

Stephen had met Pamela during the week but never mentioned the events of Sunday evening, much less chastise her for her duplicity. He and Sinead slowly got back to something approaching the close relationship they had enjoyed before the Pamela incident.

Problems with either of those girls could be tackled head-on and resolved openly but not so the thorny question of Eva Lynch. What was the state of play there? He daren't ask himself.

He had neither seen nor heard from her since that fateful night in Dublin. However, she had seldom been out of his thoughts. Not a day passed, but he wondered where she was, what she was doing and above all, whom she was doing it with. She was on his mind before he drifted into sleep each night. She was still on his mind on his waking. Perhaps she was feeling the same way and waiting on a call from him.

He had been tempted to call her mobile number. He resisted that temptation. It wasn't a fear of the call being uncovered by others but rather a dread of Eva's reaction. It was just possible that she may have regretted the encounter. Perhaps she was desperately attempting to banish it and possibly him also from her memory. Maybe some other young man had taken her fancy. Somehow he doubted this very much indeed. The bottom line was that he did not know what he wanted when it came to Eva Lynch.

All of this uncertainty and worry was having a detrimental effect on his already frayed nerves. It was bad enough having a few dozen youngsters making his daily life a misery without his social life slipping into a morass of preoccupation and frustration. Even when he was in the company of the lovely Sinead, thoughts of Eva Lynch encroached mercilessly on their time together.

Stephen's first summons to the principal's office since the mid-term break brought more headaches for the young teacher. Two of his brighter and more motivated students had transferred to another teacher. The story was that they had done so because the other teacher maintained a better learning environment. It was clear evidence that his personal problems were affecting his professional performance. Before the break, he had been drinking too much to dull the pain of the daylight hours. It was all beginning to take its toll. Class preparation had taken a back seat on his list of priorities. That only served to exacerbate the situation.

Lynch urged Stephen to knuckle down and try to rescue his floundering career. He suggested greater firmness as well as improved class preparation.

'You know, Stephen, when students are worked hard, they have less time for misbehaviour. Keep them busy, lad. You have to address yourself to this problem', Lynch added, tapping the office desk for emphasis.

He went on to point out that most parents are reasonable. They will give a teacher a chance to establish himself but the honeymoon period comes to an end.

'You have to shape up or, well, you know yourself', Lynch continued. 'Judging by your appearance and frequent lateness, you have been having too many late nights. You simply can't go on burning the candle at both ends.'

'I'll do my very best'. Stephen assured him.

'Let's hope that is enough, Lynch replied. 'I hear your love life is creating its problems too. You need to sort that out too.'

Stephen was flabbergasted. He wondered if he could be referring to Eva. He knew that this was unlikely. How could Lynch know? Eva was hardly likely to blurt it out when she got home after their rendezvous in Dublin.

'You and Ms Mc Enroe seem to have a rather curious relationship. Don't allow any relationship problems you may have to be carried over into the school'.

Simon Lynch was more informed than one might have imagined him to be.

'I think that problem has already been solved, Mr Lynch'

'I am glad to hear it. Now get out of here and show me that you are deserving of the faith that we put in you!'

'Yes, Sir!'

Nobody knew better than Stephen that he needed to improve his classroom management. But how might this improvement be managed?

The relationship with Sinead had helped keep life in perspective. She was a rock of common sense, and her support for him made life more bearable. He had always looked forward to meeting up with her. Sinead had enabled him to keep his problems in perspective.

Now, however, he was less focused on her.

That fateful night with Eva Lynch had unleashed great turmoil in his mind. He loved Sinead as much as ever and yet found it difficult

to understand his preoccupation with Eva. Whatever her appeal, one thing was becoming increasingly evident to him.
Eva Lynch was most definitely usurping Sinead in his thoughts. It was as if he was in thrall to the woman.

Stephen had become so preoccupied of late, with competing thoughts vying for supremacy in his distracted mind. The classroom had become a war zone for him. Despite the ostensibly supportive words from Lynch, he felt that he was receiving precious little in the way of support. It was a case of sink or swim as far as the principal was concerned. Unfortunately, at that moment in time, Stephen showed little ability when it came to staying afloat.

It had been yet another late night. Earlier in the school year, Stephen would never drink more than a glass or two of lager during the working week.
Recently, however, he had broken many hitherto golden rules. He was a young man under pressure. This pressure was beginning to take its toll.

A heavy drink-induced sleep resulted in Stephen sleeping in until ten minutes to nine. Then, having no time for breakfast or shaving, he carelessly threw on his tobacco-scented clothes, hopelessly trying to make school on time.
Tom was not timetabled to start for another hour yet.
For one tantalising moment, he toyed with the idea of taking Tom's car. He could not find the keys anywhere, so he set out on foot rather than waste time searching for them. Even though the car might have brought him on time, it would probably have triggered a major row with his friend. It was perhaps a good thing that he couldn't locate the keys as Tom was uncharacteristically prickly, a condition which Stephen attributed to girlfriend trouble.

At ten past nine, Stephen Daly raced towards his second-floor classroom. Climbing the terrazzo staircase, he was lucky to escape a shower of spit, which rained down from a floor above him. This spitting was one of the more vulgar and disgusting practices perpetrated by some of the low life of St. Jude's.
The terrazzo stairway, stained and streaked by saliva, bore testimony to the long-established nature of this loathsome conduct. It was extremely difficult to apprehend the guilty parties in this cowardly and

reprehensible behaviour. The delinquents, on this occasion, were from his class as they were the only ones still unsupervised at this time. There was nothing to be gained by even commenting on it. Nobody would admit to doing it as nobody would rat on a classmate. The students would stare at him blankly as if they had no idea what he was talking about.

When he finally made his way to his door, the horseplay eased. It was not that they feared chastisement. They simply wanted to enjoy his reaction to the surprise they had in store for him. They observed him closely as he put his key into the lock. His key would not turn the lock. Once again, the lock had been deliberately stuffed. Broken matches combined with hard-set chewing gum had seen to that. Derisive laughter rose from the assembled swarm of students buzzing around Stephen as he tried in vain to turn the key.

The noise level increased.

'Is this a free class, Sir?'

'Can we go to the Study Hall?'

One or two more interested students offered assistance in freeing the lock, assistance that went unappreciated by the clear majority.

'I have a compass, Sir.'

'No, you don't', said his angry-looking friend. 'Remember, you lost it yesterday.'

The lad, who had offered the compass, unconvincingly remembered that he had, after all no compass to offer the teacher.

'Will we go to the Study Hall'?

Jimmy Corrigan, who was attempting to teach in the adjacent classroom, came to investigate the disorder. He had initially imagined that Stephen had once again failed to show. However, on seeing his friend, he strolled over to him.

'Stephen, you better send them down to the Study Hall until the door is sorted out. You know the score. There will be complaints from some of the cranks around here if this racket lasts much longer.'

Stephen signalled to his class to go down quietly to the supervised Study Hall. They departed to a chorus of cheering and roaring as they charged down the stairway, some sprawled across the handrails as they slid down.

Corrigan surveyed the younger man with some concern.

'Jaysus Stephen, you look shite. Did you sleep in those clothes?

He moved to settle the upturned collar on Stephen's shirt.

'And the smell of stale beer would knock down an elephant. Have you any mints at all?'

'No, I don't. Is it that bad?'

Corrigan did not answer but went to check if he had any in his coat pocket.

Corrigan's class had now begun to hum, but his reappearance in the classroom remedied that situation

Stephen stroked the stubble on his face and contemplated the pathetic sight he was projecting to the world. He flattened his hair with the back of his hand and straightened his tie. Corrigan returned, having located a packet of *Polo* mints.

'Sinead must be very demanding. A good rest is what you need. Some time out of bed would do you a power of good', he joked.
'Jimmy, what I need and what I can get are two very different things. Give me a hand with this door lock. The stupid fuckers, they don't even realise that it's their own time they're wasting.'

Corrigan returned to his classroom to borrow a compass from a student there. After about five or six minutes of prodding and teasing at the lock, they managed to remove the cause of the problem.
'I wonder should I get the class back from the Study Hall now?' he asked the older man.
'Leave them where they are. You wouldn't even have them settled before the bell.'
Corrigan was right.
Stephen opted to go down to the staff room and make a strong cup of coffee for himself. His stomach rumbled for the want of a good breakfast.
At lunchtime, Stephen nipped back to the house for a shave and a shower. He also managed a change of clothes.
Coming out of the shower, he felt clean and refreshed, as if he had washed the morning right out of his system.
He hoped that Lynch had not checked the attendance sheet in the Study Hall.
If he did, then he was in more trouble. He dreaded yet another summons to the office. Even Stephen himself privately conceded that Simon Lynch could hardly have acted differently. A model young teacher, he certainly wasn't.

In the afternoon, Stephen's freshly groomed appearance did not go unnoticed by Jimmy Corrigan.

'You scrub up well. Are you going teaching or courting?'

'I'm courting disaster, most likely. I think it's my mother's fault for christening me, Stephen' I'm a bloody martyr'.

'And like Saint Stephen, you know what it's like to be stoned', Corrigan joked.

'But tell me this; how you got on with the boss? Did he show you the yellow card?'

Stephen briefed Jimmy Corrigan on his meeting with the principal. Jimmy felt Lynch's attitude had been patronising in the extreme. Still, Stephen accepted that any principal would be within his rights to terminate his contract for such unprofessional behaviour.

After school, Stephen and Jimmy were having their usual cup of coffee in the staff room.

Simon Lynch and Ellen Hayes were relaxing over a cup of tea. It looked as if she was settling in for the evening. Lynch pointedly complimented Stephen on his improved appearance before sitting down alongside Ellen Hayes. He handed her some literature about retreats and had a few confidential remarks with her.

Ellen Hayes was a changed woman. She was looking noticeably smarter than she had looked for a long time. She seemed to be taking new pride in her appearance. Her hair, which had suffered from chronic neglect, had recently been styled. Even her clothes took on a brighter hue indicative of a more cheerful disposition. Blue had become the new black for her.

Jimmy joked that Ellen might have a toyboy hidden away somewhere in her house.

Whatever the reason for her newfound joie- de–vivre, people were genuinely happy for her.

A faint ringing sound awakened Stephen from his sleep in the early hours of a late November morning. It took him several moments for the source of the ringing to register with him. Eventually, he traced it to his mobile phone, which was charging on a nearby chair. His watch informed him that it was 2.15 a.m. He wondered why anyone might be ringing him at that hour. He hoped that it was not bad news. There had been more than enough of that already. Maybe it was some students at an all-night session.

He dreaded the notion that some of them had got hold of his mobile number. It was bad enough that they were ringing the landline. His first reaction was to switch off the phone. However, curiosity got the better of him.

The display screen informed him that the caller's number was being withheld.

He instantly recognised the voice at the other end.

'Eva, where on earth are you? What's the problem?' he asked, his eyes still half-closed in sleep. 'Are you stuck somewhere?'

'No, nothing like that, but I do need to talk to you soon'.

She apologised for calling so late, but it seemed to offer the best chance of a private chat. She explained that she was ringing from the bedroom of her hotel in Donegal.

She wanted him to know that she would be at home in Castlehome by about three o'clock on the following day. Simon was scheduled to be in Dublin at a principals' meeting and would not be home until eight o'clock. Stephen could call after school when they could have a quiet chat. Stephen knew that a quiet chat was the last thing on her mind.

Nevertheless, he could not help himself. He thought for a moment but agreed to this proposed arrangement and wished her sweet dreams. Her call had put an end to his sleep for the night as his mind kept tossing and turning. He fondly recalled their night together in that Dublin hotel. Not surprisingly, he wished that he might somehow be transported to that Donegal hotel.

He found it more difficult than usual to get through school the next day. He rehearsed over and over what he would say to Eva and wondered even more what she might have to say to him. He could not figure out whether it was a good sign or a bad sign that she was still awake at such an hour. He was angry with her for seemingly ignoring him in the interim yet feeling unsettled because she had rung him.

After school, Stephen went home to freshen up. He usually showered after work to flush away the demons of the day. However, on this occasion, he did everything short of exfoliating and shaving his legs.

He also got into the habit of shaving after the evening meal. Typically, he had a very noticeable five o'clock shadow. Designer stubble held no attraction for him. Whatever about how it may have looked on him, it made him feel very grubby.

Like a good army general, he meticulously planned every manoeuvre. Suspecting that someone might see him at Lynch's door, he chose to carry a folder in his hand. To any casual observer, it would look like a school-related visit.

When he arrived, the front door was slightly ajar. A strangely subdued looking Eva Lynch ushered Stephen inside. She directed him into a

sitting room where the television was blaring away, unwatched. The room presented a very cosy picture with curtains drawn and a real coal fire glowing in the hearth. A half-finished mug of coffee and the remains of a toasted sandwich rested on a glass-topped table.
Stephen politely declined what seemed to him a half-hearted offer of a cup of coffee.

Eva looked away from him as she nervously directed a question towards him.
'Stephen, have you ever thought of me since that night at Halloween?'
Before he could answer, she continued.
'Because I have done little else but think of you. I have tried to get you out of my mind, but I can't.'
Stephen wasn't sure how to react, so he remained silent while she continued.
'I must admit that I expected you to make some contact in the interim'.
Her face was vainly searching his for some promise of hope.
He had rehearsed many scenarios in his mind, but he had not envisaged this particular one.
When he finally spoke, his words came from his heart rather than from his memory.
'Of course, I've thought of you. What more could I do but think? I have qualms of conscience about what we are doing.' He waited for her response. When it did not come, he continued with his explanation.
'I couldn't exactly call up to the house. You're a married woman, after all. And you're married to my boss. Anyway, how was I to know that you'd be interested in seeing me again?'

Eva, although feeling slighted, was relieved to hear that Stephen had at least thought of her.
He admitted that he had thought of little else but her. Yet, he had felt frustrated and helpless. His work had suffered, as indeed had his whole general attitude and even appearance. The uncertainty regarding her feelings served only to compound matters.
She listened as he explained how he vainly attempted to banish thoughts of her from his tormented mind and how he repeatedly reminded himself that the relationship was doomed.
Yet, the rational part of him had proved the weaker part. When Eva's phone call came, he readily confessed that he was drooling at the prospect of another sizzling encounter. This woman had violently hijacked his emotions and propelled his hormones into a veritable tizzy.

Eva was grateful that the door of hope had not been completely shut on her, and she visibly relaxed. The worried expression gradually lifted from her face. These last few moments answered questions, which had haunted them both. It was as if they had turned a page in their relationship.
It was also apparent that there was more to their relationship than purely physical attraction. Neither had a clearly defined notion of what this relationship would involve or even the direction it might take them. However, both desperately wanted the relationship to continue. It was not going to be easy. Both had much to lose. This affair had to be kept secret. Stephen and Eva agreed that they would meet when

circumstances permitted. No unnecessary risks were to be taken by either. Snatched moments were all they could hope for.

With what passed for ground rules established, for the moment anyway, the atmosphere noticeably lightened. Leaning back on the sofa, Eva kicked off her shoes and stretched her feet across his welcoming lap.

'Come on, give my feet a nice massage; I've been on them all day'.

'Sole-destroying!' punned Stephen, the tension in him slowly dissipating. Eva smiled, but in a moment, the tears appeared.

'Hold me, Stephen! Please hold me. I need to be held.'

Taking her in his arms, he held her close to him and gently stroked her cheek, reassuring her that everything would now be fine.

On that fateful night in Dublin, Eva was the stronger of the two. She was the one who gave direction and the one who seemed so very confident and self-assured. Now it was Stephen's turn to be the stronger one. In many ways, their roles had now been reversed. Now, she was the nervous one. He seemed to be the one who knew what he wanted and did not want.

'Stephen, I dreaded your reaction this evening. I imagined that you would tell me to get lost, that you wanted nothing to do with a middle-aged woman like me.'

He assured her that age was not an issue for him. He lied.

The embrace, which comforted Eva unintentionally, served as the prelude to greater intimacies. Eva dimmed the recessed lights on the ceiling and switched off the television. She took Stephen by the hand, leading him onto the floral patterned, oriental rug in front of the open fire. A few moments later, their bodies lay entangled on that same rug. The flickering shadows on the wall moved to their rhythm while the fire sparked its warm approval.

For a considerable time afterwards, Stephen lay alongside Eva beside the warm hearth. Disparate thoughts raced heedlessly through his receptive mind. He tried to imagine Simon Lynch, flat-footedly, retiring to this room after a demanding day in the principal's office. He visualised Eva and Lynch sitting together on the sofa and wondered whether she had ever seductively led him to the warm hearth. He further questioned whether he was even the first young Castlehome teacher to sample the thrills of that hearth.

He was suddenly reminded of Sinead. He had arranged to meet her at Taylor's at ten o'clock. He felt bad about cheating on Sinead, but for some reason, he did not feel guilt. He rationalised that he had been more a passive agent than an active participant in shaping and directing events. It felt good to be with Eva Lynch, but Sinead was still his girl despite the thrills he had experienced with the older woman.

Eva was keen to arrange their next tryst. However, few possibilities readily presented themselves. Finally, it was agreed that as she would be staying over in Dublin on the following Sunday night, that offered the safest or most attractive option. The plan was that Stephen would take himself off home for the weekend. This arrangement was fast becoming an attractive proposition. On Sunday night, he would take a taxi to her hotel in Ballsbridge. Then having spent the night with Eva and he would take the red-eye express to Castlehome. If all went to plan, he would have time to drop his bags home and be in class for nine forty-five. As it happened, Monday was one of the two days when he was free for the first class period.

Christmas was coming, and the turkeys were beginning to get fat and nervous. With the holidays within sight, there was a reason for optimism. In racing parlance, they were in the final furlong of a very challenging course. Sinead suggested that they should organise a party. Such a party would be a fitting end to what had been a troubled year. She volunteered Number 22 as the venue. It made the most sense. Sinead and her nursing colleague Susan would arrange to be off duty on whatever night was decided upon for the party. The guests would be requested to bring along their own drinks, while they would organise some bites.

While Sinead and Pamela were not exactly bosom pals, they had learned to cohabit in a reasonably civilised manner. Their different working hours meant that they had very little social contact. Sinead was excited as she contemplated the arrangements.

December 12 seemed the best night.

'It will be the last Friday night, which will suit the teachers and Susan and I will be free on that Saturday. I'll ask a few more of the girls from the hospital. We'll have a good party. What will we do for music?'

Stephen wasn't convinced of the need for such planning. The best parties were always the impromptu ones.

'We have plenty of CDs. Anyway, if we are stuck, Tom can bring his guitar.'

'I suppose you're right,' conceded Sinead. 'By the way, is Tom still going with that Linda girl from the Post Office?'

'I believe he is, Sinead, but it's hard to keep track of what he's up to or who the unfortunate girl is'.

Sinead still pushed Stephen on this question. She could not understand that he didn't have a better idea of what his flatmate was up to.

'Well, do you know what Susan Kelly is up to? Do you? You always tell me how private she can be'.

'Point taken', acknowledged Sinead as Stephen elaborated.

'Tom and I may be best of friends, but he does not confide in me.'

As Stephen reflected on the year just ending, it was not all despair and depression. He had passed his university exams. He had come to Castlehome, a place that he was growing to love. He had made some very good friends, and of course, he had met the twin passions of his romantic life there.

The year had its good points as well as its bad points.

But deep down, he knew that the basics were all wrong.

In class, he was still a disaster. His drinking was even giving his friends cause for concern. While Sinead was, for some reason, distant and preoccupied, Eva was driving him crazy with lust. Things would inevitably come to a head. In a moment or two, the door opened with the arrival of Tom Clarke.

'Talk of the devil', shouted Stephen as he called his friend to join them.

Tom strolled over to their table, slapping a few backs on his way and scanning the crowd for other familiar faces.

'What will you have, Tom? It's my shout', insisted Stephen, reaching into his pocket.

'Sinead was just wondering if you are still shifting that Linda girl'.

'I was not', protested an injured Sinead, who once again reddened with embarrassment. 'Don't heed him. He's just curious.'

Tom shrugged his shoulders, debating whether he would update them or not.
'Well, if you must know, we broke up last weekend. There was nothing there, and we both knew it. Look to the future and better women. That's my motto', he said.
'No better man to line up a replacement,' remarked Stephen.
Tom chose to ignore that remark.
'What will I get for you? A pint of the usual?'
'Yeah, go on. That would be great.'
As he waited for the drinks to fill, Stephen could see that Tom and Sinead seemed to be having a private chat. He couldn't make out what they were talking about, but they looked very much at ease and interested in what the other had to say. Both threw the odd glance in Stephen's direction, something that unnerved him. He suspected that they were commenting on his drinking. He had enough of that and hoped that he could be his true self with them.
When Stephen returned with the drink, Tom turned the conversation to the forthcoming school talent competition. He jokingly suggested to Stephen that there should be a staff section to the talent show.

He imagined Ellen Hayes doing a bit of belly dancing and maybe Jimmy Corrigan singing some *Spice Girls* hit.
'What about yourself, Stephen? What will I put you down for? Will it be a recitation or maybe a verse or two of *The Rocky Road to Dublin*?'
'Tom, I know my limitations. I think that if there were a singing competition among the staff, it would be a straight fight between you and Simon Lynch'.

Tom was not flattered by being mentioned in such a company.
'I feel certain I'd get a walkover in that case. What talent has that fucker?'
Stephen nudged Sinead before he answered.
'Funny Tom, but he said the same about you, on the morning he caught you in your undies singing on the staffroom table.'
'Very funny, Daly; you are very funny. Only that you are such a dozy bastard, you'd have heard him coming and warned me'.

Stephen laughed heartily to himself. Only when pushed by Sinead and Tom, did he admit that he heard footsteps approaching that fateful morning. He had no idea who was on the way but thought it would be a bit of gas if some old prude like Ellen Hayes had walked in.
'Some bloody friend, you are', said Tom in disgust.
'I was there making a complete fool of myself, and this fucker lets the principal walk in on me. How could you have been so cruel?'
'Tom, you have to believe me. I had no idea it was Lynch. If I had known it, I would have tipped you off. You don't think that I'd ever do anything to assist that old fart. But you have to admit that if it were Ellen, you'd be dining out on the story for weeks'.

Tom was unimpressed with Stephen's justification of his perceived betrayal.
'Don't be trying to wriggle out of it, Daly. You set me up good and proper but wait yet! Some day, when you least expect it, I'll get my own back on you. Then we'll see who's laughing?'
'Oh', said Stephen feigning great trepidation.

'I must check your location before I sing into a broom handle while half-naked on a table. Sinead, remind me about that', he said, nudging his girlfriend with his elbow.

'Not a pretty sight, Sinead, seeing this fellow half-naked on a table', ventured Tom.

Sinead felt distinctly uncomfortable with that particular line of conversation.

'God, you are so immature, the two of you. Together, you wouldn't make one proper man. Let me out of here. I suddenly feel the need to go to the toilet. The two of you, you piss me off, do you know that?'

As she wound her way through the crowd, the two boys looked at each other in total amazement.

'What's up with Sinead?' asked Tom. 'She's so bloody touchy tonight'.

'I don't know. The girl is in bad form, I'd say'.

'Whatever it is, I'm sure I will get the sharp edge of it soon'.

The annual Student Talent Night in the college assembly hall was the highlight of the students' year. The assembly hall would typically be packed to the rafters with students, parents and friends of the contestants. The adjudicators were invariably respected figures from the local musical or dramatic scene.

On the night of the contest, all the teachers were involved in some way or another. Some had volunteered for set construction, others for supervisory duties, while a few were engaged in ushering. Stephen and Corrigan had volunteered to take the admission fee at the door.

For students attending single-sex schools, a night such as this was a rare opportunity to come into close contact with large numbers of the opposite sex. Consequently, there is always an element of danger associated with such occasions. There was no predicting what an individual might do to impress his peers.

The first item on the programme was a musical act for the culture vultures: *Shades of Mozart.* It was a trio of First-year students earnestly playing some classical composition that was unknown to Stephen and the overwhelming majority of those present. The trio featured a piano, violin and what Stephen judged to be a cello. The performers were competent musicians, but their music was not appreciated by the audience. If there ever was a case of casting pearls before swine, this was it.

Their performance was greeted with jeering, booing and something approaching bowel sounds. Teachers who were positioned along the sides of the hall bravely attempted to stifle such responses. Still, under cover of darkness, it was all too easy for the hecklers to continue unidentified.

The second act of the night was listed in the programme as being a comedy act. In a way, it was comical, but not for the intended reasons. The poor unfortunate lad was so distracted by the catcalling and heckling that he forgot his script. He succeeded in remembering some of his material but had trouble preserving the sequence and remembering his punch lines. He began to panic. Then, rather than present a dumb show, he opted to recite poetry. The only work that he could recall was a poem that Stephen had taught in class. The elegy *Thomas Mc Donagh,* which commemorates the 1916 leader, would hardly spring to mind when one thought of comedy.

But it was a case of any port in a storm.

The novelty act of the night featured what could only very loosely be described as a ventriloquist. This chancer had gone to the full rounds as regards presentation and props. Dressed in a black tuxedo with a contrasting white frilly shirt and bow tie, his dummy looked more human than he did. Cheekily, he named his dummy *Simple Simon.* The audience rightly took this as a thinly veiled send-up of their beloved headmaster. The routine was in itself quite funny. The central character was a wooden dummy dressed up in a tweed jacket and red tie.

Amazingly, he just happened to be called Simon. At least they didn't give him the principal's surname. Apparently, Simon had got too big for his boots and had to get a new pair. He kept shouting swear words, which the ventriloquist would vainly pretend to stifle. Even though Stephen was standing well down the hall, he could see the ventriloquist's lips moving. They would hardly have moved more in normal conversation. This student had quite limited career prospects in the entertainment industry unless ventriloquism suddenly became a popular radio act.

The following acts were largely ignored as all the attention was focused on anticipating the heavy rock bands to come. They performed under such genteel names as *Puke* and *Spit.* Any relationship between their performance and music would be very difficult to prove in a court of law. Essentially, it was a discordant combination of head-splitting noise, mangling of guitar strings into an ear-assailing cacophony. This was associated with some rather violent, circular head movements. There was the occasional identifiable sound in the lyrics. The audience was regularly urged to 'Chill out' and 'Get in the groove.'

Many of the younger audience responded like Pavlovian dogs. They leapt to their feet in a near frenzied state and manifested what can only be described as an involuntary muscular movement. At this stage, the entire assembly hall was deliriously throbbing with the good vibrations. The very building seemed to pulsate. Those of more mature years looked at each other, hands over their ears with painful expressions on their faces.

At half-past ten, the contest had reached its conclusion. The adjudicators had just returned from an understandably short conference in an unheated classroom within the same block.

Before the result was announced, Mr Simon Lynch attempted to address the audience. He had intended to thank the audience for their presence and support. However, he was the wrong man in the wrong place at the wrong time.

Derisive shouts of: 'Get off the stage', competed with calls for the return of Puke.

Lynch decided that discretion was the better part of valour. The best thing for him to do was to announce the result. While it was originally intended that there be just one winner of the contest, the judging panel was well aware that they still had to get out of the hall. Therefore, one of the rock bands had to feature in the prize money.

After some brief conferring, the foreman of adjudicating panel announced the result.

The joint winners were the classical trio *Shades of Mozart* and *Puke.*

'And I thought they were the same thing', laughed Stephen.

It had been a morning of thundery downpours, which continued until mid-afternoon. Any time heavy rain fell over lunchtime, there would invariably be requests from opportunistic students to be allowed to sign out and go home. Many of those would have deliberately walked out in the rain to get a good soaking. They were always likely to be disappointed in such a request. The principal had repeatedly made it clear that signing out would not be an option in such circumstances. Parents had been urged to invest in rain gear for the boys. Many parents did as requested, but their sons stubbornly refused to don the waterproof gear. They seemed to consider it unmanly to cover up during a deluge, even if that meant sitting for hours in soaked clothes and spongy footwear.

Stephen was teaching his Fourth Year class on Wednesday afternoon. He had slowly begun to build a relationship with this group of lads. The majority of the students were a pleasure to deal with. However, the more difficult ones took up so much teaching time and constantly frustrated him.

When four such drenched students arrived at his door some ten minutes late for that period, he resented the interruption. He had earlier observed the quartet coming from behind the bicycle shed, a notorious hangout for smokers. No doubt they had also called to the office in a vain attempt to be allowed to sign out. Wandering the streets in the lashing rain would be seen as much more appealing than sitting in his classroom learning about Shakespeare's *Macbeth.*

Stephen Daly demanded an explanation.

'You are late, boys. What have you to say for yourselves?'

One muttered something about remaining under a tree, hoping for the rain to ease, but that was patent nonsense. The others just looked down, waiting for the moment to pass. The strong smell of tobacco from all four suggested that they had been smoking.

He could accuse them of doing so, but there was little point in making a big issue of it. What would follow would be the inevitable denials, which would only serve to waste more class time.

'Go on, take a seat and don't let this happen again.'

Before he proceeded with the main business of the class, there were compositions to be returned. For the previous weekend, the boys had been assigned an essay. Stephen had been systematically working his way through the different styles of essay from the examination paper. For the weekend, the boys had to write under the heading *Memories*. Students were encouraged to view the title in its broadest sense. He also wished to integrate other aspects of the course. As the class had earlier worked on sensuous descriptions in poetry, he suggested that the boys include descriptions of sights, sounds, and even smells when appropriate.

Most had interpreted the title in the narrowest sense. Nevertheless, Stephen had been impressed by the standard of writing. By and large, they had observed his guidelines as regards structure. It was rewarding to feel that he was making progress with the group. However, there is always one student who prefers to take the effortless route. Eamon O'Neill, a likeable student, was one of that number. Today Stephen intended to have fun at that lad's expense, and he had come prepared.

O' Neill's essay caused Stephen to laugh out loud when he read it. He had shown it to his colleague Tom, who admired the boy's audacity. Stephen feigned admiration and respect for Eamon's contribution. He spoke of a remarkable essay that had been written by one of the class. He then identified Eamon O'Neill as the author of the outstanding piece.

The other boys looked around with a mixture of amazement and perplexity. Finally, Stephen invited the young man to read the first paragraph of his work aloud to the class.

Initially, Eamon seemed unsure but slowly appeared to revel in his newfound status as an author of substance. Then, being anything but reticent, he cleared his throat and began to read.

I remember that summer in Dublin, and the Liffey as it stank like hell,
And the young people walking on Grafton Street, and everyone looking so well,
I was singing a song I heard somewhere, called "Rock 'n' roll never forgets",
When my hummin' was smothered by a 46a and the scream of a low flying jet.

Eamon took a bow before sitting down to the sound of his classmates' applause ringing in his ears.

Stephen joined in the applause. Like an expert fisherman, he had got his target to bite and was playing him on the line until he was ready to go in for the kill. He dissected the poetic turn of phrase, line by line.

He made particular reference to the descriptions of sights, sounds, and indeed smells.
Eamon was enjoying his moment in the spotlight. However, that was soon to change as Stephen went one step further in his praise of the piece.
'In fact, your essay is so good that it might well be published as a poem or a song.

The poor lad was beginning to look a little uncomfortable. He seemed to suspect that he was about to be exposed as a chancer.
'In fact, I have a strong feeling that somebody may have already turned it into a song'. Stephen proceeded to press the PLAY button on the CD player, which he had brought to class with him. In a moment, singer-songwriter, Liam Reilly and *Bagatelle* blasted out those very words to the puzzled class.
Eamon had been outed for his plagiarism.
The other boys really enjoyed their classmate's discomfort.
'Sickened! Sickened! You were got good and proper, O'Neill'
The young student reddened with embarrassment.

Stephen had no intention of making a big issue over what was essentially a bit of fun.
The student had been caught out in deception, but it was not of any great significance.
Even Eamon could see that his teacher was more amused than angry.
'I am surprised that you even know that song? Stephen said.
'And I am even more than surprised that you knew it, Sir'.
Both laughed heartily at that remark.

'Anyway, my dad is from Dublin, and he often sings it'.
"Eamon, tell the lads what the song is called'?'
'The title is *Summer in Dublin'*.
'It is indeed, and you have done an excellent job in transcribing another man's lyrics. I hope you do as good a job on your own. I want to see your proper essay on my desk Friday morning'.

It was time to get back to the serious business of the class. The boys had already spent some time on the tragedy *Macbeth*, so the boys were familiar with the plot. Inevitably the archaic language posed enormous problems for them.
'Sir, why don't they speak proper English like us?'
Stephen did his best to explain how language changes over time, but the boys had quickly lost interest.
There was one television and video player for the entire floor. Teachers had to book the video in advance. Then, they had to retrieve it from its storage room and wheel it and the TV over on a trolley to their classrooms. The trolley was a bit unsteady as one of the back wheels was missing.
Nevertheless, it was better than nothing. Stephen was glad that he had managed to book the video for that particular class period.

He switched on the video and turned out the room lights
Thanks to the overcast conditions, the class could see the screen reasonably clearly.
Stephen explained that he would allow the video to run for twenty minutes before pausing to explain some notable points and take any

questions. That was all very well in theory, but some individuals were unable to accept that discipline.

One innocent lad asked:

'Did those soldiers know that they were being filmed?'

Stephen looked at him in disbelief and wondered how he might best deal with that question. However, his classmates were less considerate as they ridiculed him for his question.

'Jaysus, Finnegan thinks they had cameras covering the big battles in the eleventh century'.

'Finnegan, you are even more stupid than you look, and that takes some doing.

'Now, that's enough, boys. I just said that we would watch the video for twenty minutes. After that, there would be an opportunity for you to ask your questions'.

The boys looked at him as if they resented any restrictions on their spontaneity.

The video continued to play. It was clear that the bloody and gruesome battle scenes gripped the class.

'There was a lot of tomato ketchup used up there.'

'Better than Brave Heart', another lad remarked to his friend.

After twenty minutes elapsed, Stephen again paused the video.

'Now, I will take any questions'.

Most of the boys had forgotten what they had intended to ask.

One or two had questions.

'Are there witches today, Sir?'

Before Stephen could answer, there came a shouted answer from the back of the room.

'Yes, and she teaches us Religion'.

'Next question?'

'What would Macbeth be earning as a soldier?'

Stephen had not been expecting such a question. Nevertheless, he explained that Macbeth was a lord who owned a very large estate. He was loyal to his king, so he fought out of a sense of duty to Duncan. Furthermore, he reminded the class that even though Duncan was not an effective ruler, he was still the boss and had to be obeyed and supported.

'A bit like Lynch in his school', a lad astutely remarked.

Another lad asked quite seriously why King Duncan did not seem to own a television set.

Once again, this innocent remark unleashed a barrage of abuse from the lads, who felt that they knew better.

'You stupid bastard, how could they have television back then? They just about had a radio'.

Maybe it had been a mistake to interrupt the video at all.

'OK, I will take one more question'.

A hand shot up.

'Can I go to the toilet?'

It was time to move on with the video.

On Saturday morning Stephen Daly drove his mother into Dublin City centre. While she did some shopping, he savoured a Saturday morning browse through the department stores. His sisters, Niamh and Lorraine, were enjoying their usual Saturday morning lie-in. His father had brought some paperwork home and intended to take full advantage of the quiet surroundings.
Stephen was delighted to tramp the streets of Dublin again. Castlehome was a fine town and had much to offer. But, on the other hand, Dublin was the metropolis, and for most of his life, it was his home.

At noon, he and his mother met as per arrangement for coffee. An array of store bags testified to a successful morning's shopping. It was a time to rest tired feet and show off one's purchases.
'I thought I'd treat myself to a new top and skirt. But, then again, I couldn't leave behind this trouser suit. It was a steal at the price.' Rosaleen Daly seemed happy with her purchases. Her son was delighted for her. She pulled the jacket of the trouser suit out and asked for her son's opinion. Without even turning his head in his mother's direction, Stephen professed himself an admirer of both the colour and style. He had learned from his father that the female invariably requires approval rather than opinion in such instances.
'I am not getting any younger, but I still take pride in my appearance. And that reminds me, thanks for your birthday card last week', Rosaleen added mischievously.

Her birthday had slipped his mind. He felt so selfish and so guilty. He had always made a note of family birthdays well in advance and would have a suitable card chosen, but this year, it had gone clean out of his mind.

'Mom, I feel so bad. I just never thought.'

He buried his face in his hands, shaking his head ruefully from side to side as if to reposition the pieces responsible for his recent memory lapses.

His mother was smiling at his obvious discomfort.

'Oh, I know how it is. There's probably some other young lady who's occupying your thoughts right now. You can't be expected to remember two birthdays'.

She was enjoying his minor discomfort.

'Who is the girl?'

Stephen did not immediately answer her.

'And when will I meet her?'

Stephen shyly admitted that there was a young lady. He told her that she was a nurse and that it was in the early stages of the relationship, so there was little to report. There was no mention of Eva Lynch, however. He saw her as a creature for just the night or the half-light.

His mother wished to put him straight on a few points. There was nothing new in her message. He had heard her preach the same gospel so many times before.

'Now, Stephen, remember to treat her properly. Don't forget what I always told you', she added, warming to her subject.

'And don't come home here telling me that you've got her pregnant. I don't want to be a granny yet.'
'You're too young to be a granny anyway; you don't look the part'. Rosaleen was adamant.
'I was forty-seven on Tuesday', she admitted. 'Mary Kelly, over in Swan Avenue is forty-five, and she became a granny in August, thanks to that brat of a son of hers.'
Stephen knew Mary well and knew her son Sean who was younger than he.
'So Sean got Sharon up the pole', mused Stephen.
'Don't be crude', she pleaded. 'It doesn't suit you'.
This conversation unexpectedly provided Stephen with much food for thought. After all, he had unprotected sex with a married woman who was as old as his mother.
Moreover, her children were within two years of leaving school. It wouldn't be outrageous to imagine a child for either in the medium term. Eva being almost a granny and he sleeping with her was certainly a sobering thought. Was he losing his marbles or what?
In the space of a few short moments of reflection, the older woman's appeal seemed to wane. It was as if the cold, searching light of realism had penetrated the romantic mists, which had shrouded Eva.
While his mother continued to lecture him on some of the younger generation's irresponsibility, Stephen's mind was attempting to tease out what exactly he felt for Eva Lynch. His gut reaction was to return to Castlehome on Sunday evening without a word to Eva, but that would be heartless as well as cowardly. On reflection, he figured that

he should at least leave a message at her hotel. That way, although still cowardly, she would not be expecting him.

During lunch that day, Stephen was noticeably quieter than usual. His sisters, always interested in pastures new, attempted to coax him into allowing them to visit Castlehome soon. They presumably hoped that he could introduce them to some of his more handsome colleagues. Life was a little too complicated for him to agree to this in the immediate future. Still, before summer arrived, he hoped to bring them on the grand tour of Castlehome.

Lorraine and Niamh were rapidly growing into young women. He supposed that Eva's twin girls were similarly blossoming into womanhood. What could they possibly make of his relationship with their mother?

Having found the number of her hotel in Ballsbridge, Stephen rang reception and left a message for Eva Lynch. A staff member would inform Eva that her friend from Castlehome would be unable to keep his appointment with her. His initial feeling was one of relief. A dreaded moment had passed without any real pain or discomfort. He wondered what Eva would make of the message. She would be smart enough to read between the lines. He could understand if Eva felt used or more likely abused, but who was it who said:

'All's fair in love and war?'

The time spent with the family meant a great deal to Stephen. The family seemed to be in good form, content with the way life was now treating them.

It had been so different in the years immediately following Conor's death. Even though Stephen was only five years of age at the time, he remembered it all too vividly. He and Conor had been inseparable. They got into all kinds of mischief together. Then tragically, one day, it was all over. Conor was dead. He had been standing in the back seat of the family car, returning from a dental appointment in Portlaoise. Another car ploughed into the back of their vehicle. Conor didn't stand a chance.

The driver of the other car was a learner driver from the south of the country. The young girl informed the court that she had been momentarily distracted while changing stations on her car radio.

Life changed for the entire Daly family in the aftermath of that fatal accident. Stephen could remember little except sad faces, sleepless nights and frayed nerves.

His grieving parents had a path worn to the doctor for prescription drugs in a vain attempt to cope with the pain of grief. His father applied for positions away from the town and all the terrible reminders that it harboured.

After a year or so, the family moved to Dublin. It was a fresh start for all of them. However, the sad reality was that the constant pain travelled with them. Over the years, his parents attempted to assume a semblance of normal life as the sharp edge of grief was somehow dulled by time. Even that proved problematic. Conor was never far from their minds or Stephen's mind either. For him, his birthday was always a day to endure. There were still too many ghosts around.

He was pleased that his mother could take some pleasure in a day's shopping in the city. She could take pride in her appearance and pick up the threads of her life, which had unravelled so horrendously. For Lorraine and Niamh, there were no such memories. They were born after the tragic accident. However, they were always conscious of an underlying depressing atmosphere in their home. They were not to know, but their arrival hastened the healing process for their parents in a small way. With these serious thoughts exercising his mind, Stephen went for a gentle stroll in the nearby park. Despite being late in the year, it was a day of bright, if weak, sunshine. Young and old had been attracted into the great outdoors. Elderly ladies and gentlemen, all muffled up against the elements, discreetly averted their eyes when uninhibited, young lovers kissed in their presence.

Love certainly made the world go round.

Looking at the old folk take advantage of what might be the last of the seasonal sunshine, Stephen wondered what life held up its sleeve for him. There were sure to be many upsets and many joys, but he hoped that he might one day look back with some pride on the life he had lived.

For better or for worse, his life was presently centred in Castlehome. He had made some good friends there, especially the lovely Sinead O'Shea. He would presumably forget all about the mad fling that was his affair with Eva.

He took the early train to Castlehome on Sunday evening, firmly believing that it was in everybody's best interests to do so.

On his return, Stephen telephoned the girls' house on the off chance that Sinead might be there. As it happened, she had finished work at eight o 'clock, grabbed a quick shower and was settling down to a night in front of the television, clad only in her dressing gown. She was surprised to hear from Stephen as he had given her the impression that he would not be back until the following morning.

Within a few minutes, she had dressed and had her makeup applied, ready to join Stephen in the pub.

They had little difficulty finding a table, opting to occupy a dimly lit recess. Tom Clarke was strumming on his guitar, lost in the sentiments of the song he was singing.

He nodded a greeting as they passed in front of him. Tom was glad to see them. At least he would have someone to chat to during breaks in his performance. Sinead was not pressing for an explanation for her boyfriend's unexpectedly early return. She had a long and busy day. Afterwards, it was pleasurable to unwind in restful surroundings.

Sinead held Stephen's hand gently as she snuggled close to him. Whether he was interested or not, she updated him on the goings-on at the hospital. The good news was that she had sorted out an issue with an unpleasant superior. On the other hand, she was surprisingly shocked at the suspected intimacy between two medical colleagues, a young single doctor and a married ward sister.

'Imagine having an affair with a woman nearly old enough to be your mother. No doubt, Sigmund Freud would have something to say about that.'

Maybe it was the workings of a guilty conscience. Still, as Stephen saw it, the same Sigmund Freud and his controversial views were being afforded a little too much respect.

Eva Lynch was never far from his mind that evening. Sinead's remark had brought her right to the fore again. He found it difficult to have clarity on what exactly he felt about Eva. Part of him wished he were still in Dublin with her, but another part preferred to be with Sinead. Despite what she had just said, he felt no shame attached to dating an older woman. Stephen was confused. Where had the common sense and clarity of yesterday gone? Why had he run like a frightened rabbit from an arranged meeting with Eva? These questions remained unanswered as he listened absentmindedly to Sinead's stories from Castlehome Regional Hospital. Finally, sensing that his attention was drifting, Sinead enquired about his weekend.

He told how he had spent Saturday morning on a shopping trip with his mother. Then, for some reason, he made up a story of hitting up with an old college buddy.

'Stephen, I'd love to go shopping in Dublin before Christmas. It would be so romantic, arm in arm through the Grafton Street hordes, with the lights twinkling in the frosty air, while we snuggle up together. What do you say?'

Sinead's face was already beaming at the prospect, so there was no denying this request. He promised to take her to Dublin next weekend. They could also take in a visit to a nightclub. A trip to the Dublin Mountains or down to Wicklow might be a good idea, but he realised how difficult it would be to get her away from the shops.

He knew that his mother would only be too happy to put Sinead up for a night or two. Only yesterday, she had been inquiring about his love life. Both mother and girlfriend would get along just fine, especially if let loose in the city centre together. They would travel together on the early train on Saturday morning. As Sinead was on duty on Friday evening, they would just have one night in Dublin.

Tom had taken a break from the music and had joined them at the table. Judging from the pint glass in his hand, he intended to lubricate his vocal cords.

'Can I get you anything?' Tom enquired as to their need for a refill.

They both replied in unison. 'No, thanks, we're fine'.

Tom made himself comfortable, dragging over a spare bar stool to support his feet. Stephen had seen little of Tom recently, even though they worked together and shared the same house. It was a pity because he always enjoyed Tom's company. They could be carelessly juvenile together, as Tom was generally good for a laugh. However, recently things had begun to change. They were both very busy living their own lives.

Tom assured Stephen that he had missed precious little while being out of town for the weekend. He told him that Jimmy Corrigan had been in the pub on Friday night with his sister and brother in law, who were both down from Dublin for the weekend. Corrigan had been knocking back the drinks and seemed to be in rare, good form. Inevitably the conversation turned to the coming week at school. Both men hoped Lynch might agree to a half-day to recognise the school's success in the provincial debating competition. Such a prospect was adjudged to be unlikely, but it might be an idea to start a rumour of a half-day. Nothing ventured, nothing gained.

As soon as Tom had returned to his microphone, Sinead was again planning the trip to Dublin. She was looking forward to it, as she had not shopped in the capital city for ages. It was high time she gave her credit card a vigorous workout. Her mind was already in the clothes shops, as she made a mental list of areas in which her wardrobe urgently needed enhancement. She especially needed a winter coat. She also needed a new outfit for her cousin's wedding in the New Year. Stephen smiled indulgently, envying her the enthusiasm, which she so charmingly displayed. His mind was also in Dublin. In his case, however, it did not venture any further than a Dublin 4 hotel bedroom.

As last orders were called, Stephen approached the bar to fortify himself with a double whiskey in addition to a 'Same Again' order. He wanted to guarantee himself a night's sleep.
Otherwise, he feared that his mind would be assailed with reproachful and guilt-ridden thoughts of a disillusioned and embittered Eva.
Sinead reminded the boys about the upcoming party in her house on December 12. Stephen kissed her good night at her doorway and returned home with Tom.

It was Tom Clarke's loud and repeated knocking on the door that awakened Stephen. Unfortunately, he had forgotten to set his alarm clock. Thankfully, Tom had been on hand to do the necessaries. Raising his head ever so delicately, Stephen opened his unwilling eyelids and attempted to focus on his surroundings. He had slept fully-clothed on top of the bed, onto which he had so wretchedly collapsed some seven and half hours earlier.

The sickening smell of stale beer, together with the stench of cigarette smoke, vied for supremacy with the invasive smell of urine. A quick inspection confirmed Stephen's worst fears. The therapeutic measures of whiskey may have banished sleep-inhibiting thoughts, but it had its unwelcome side effects. His fully fuelled bladder was on automatic pilot and opted to de-fuel with the result that he now found himself soaked in urine.

Stephen was mortally embarrassed. It had been years since he had been as drunk. At least the damage was mercifully confined to his trousers. The fact that he had not been under the bedclothes meant that they had emerged relatively unscathed.
By now, his sodden trousers were becoming very cold to the touch. Standing up to remove them, he stumbled and fell back onto the bed. As he undressed completely, he shivered in the cold air of the morning. After three minutes in a hot shower, he was beginning to feel a little more human again. But, of course, no one must know about his little accident; he still had his pride.

Taking his trousers, he bundled them into a supermarket bag before tossing them into the bottom of the wardrobe. There was a washing machine in the house, but he did not even know how to operate it. His housemates availed of the local laundry services, but he would be too self-conscious to show up with a pair of trousers, heavily scented with stale urine. Instead, he would have a go at washing them in the kitchen sink when the lads were out. At least a good soaking would remove the smell. Then, he could dry them on the radiator in his room. He thanked God that the duvet was dry and the mattress unaffected. Otherwise, he would be sleeping with the stench of urine for months. It would certainly give a new meaning to being on the piss every night.

In the kitchen, Tom was finishing his breakfast with one eye on Breakfast TV.

He glanced at Stephen and enquired as to his fitness for school.

'I can always say that you're feeling unwell'.

'No, Tom, I'll struggle in. You can't have old Misery Guts complaining again. Being sick on Monday is always a bit dodgy, especially when you're not permanent.'

Tom prevailed on Stephen to take a large mug of black coffee. The strong beverage brought back some colour to his cheeks but did nothing to remove the stale smell of alcohol from his breath.

'We'll stop off for the newspapers you told me to remind you about in the corner shop and get you a packet of strong mints. Don't get too close to Lynch or Shaw'

It was great to get the lift to school with Tom, even if a brisk walk in the frosty air might have been more beneficial.

On arrival, Stephen considered it prudent to go straight to his classroom. Even if he no longer smelled like a brewery, the sight of a young man chewing his way through a packet of strong mints on a Monday morning told its own damning story.

The students were not so easily fooled either. Stephen was suffering from the effects of drink, and it showed. It was not the first occasion on which they witnessed their teacher in such a shameful state. Every slip-up on his part was inevitably put down to the effects of alcohol.

A Second Year English class with the infamous Martin Greene was his first class of the day. Stephen had observed them arrive for his English lesson in a very noisy and animated state.

With a resignation that comes with fatalism, Stephen started the lesson with Media Studies. Today he would concentrate on newspapers.

Stephen explained the essential difference between the tabloid and the broadsheet regarding the layout and presentation of news. To illustrate, he had an old edition of the *Irish Independent* and *The Star*. The boys were craning their necks, attempting to read the sporting headlines and eyeing the tabloid for a possible scantily dressed female. The class continued with Stephen lacking the energy or the inclination to impose his authority. Once again, he proceeded to deliver the lesson on the teaching equivalent of automatic pilot.

'The tabloid is half the broadsheet size and as such is a more convenient size for reading on public transport. However, it lacks the detail and the formal register of the broad sheet'.

The boys did not appear particularly interested in such distinctions.

'Many people are attracted by the colour and the stylish sport's coverage in the tabloid, but for people interested in serious news and current affairs, the broadsheet is more popular.'
'But that's boring, Sir, that's like watching the news on the TV.'
'Yes,' Stephen agreed. 'Younger people generally prefer the tabloid because of its colour and coverage of sport, music and television. Still, if you want to know what's going on in politics or economics, the broadsheet will provide more information.'

Stephen felt awkward explaining the links between the socio-economic group and the type of paper read. Typically, the less educated individual would opt for a tabloid because it is easier to read. In contrast, the more educated and professional classes would be more likely to read the broadsheet. There were, of course, many notable exceptions to this rule, especially in the younger age group.
Stephen asked as to which newspaper was read in the different households and the reason for the choice. The answers in the main proved to be predictable.
'The sport is far better in the tabloid'.
'Me Ma says you miss the deaths if you don't get the big paper.'
'Me Da gets the *Sunday World*, but he won't let me read it. Ma is always giving out to him about the topless girls in the newspaper'.
'Yea!' came the enthusiastic response. 'My father takes it to the toilet with him'.
Stephen noticed that the normally verbose Martin Greene was quiet on this topic.
'Well, Martin, what paper do you get in your house?'

Martin was honest. He did not know any other way.
'Sir, we don't buy any paper. My mother and father don't read anything. But Sir, during the week, my mother sends me down to Gogan's shop for two old newspapers whenever she's washed the floor. She tells me to bring the big one because it has better coverage, she says, on the wet floor like.'
Stephen was sorry for asking the question, but there was no reaction from the class. They were by now very used to Martin and his different ways.
Martin's arrival had upset the delicate balance in Stephen Daly's class. Still, he had restored that balance in a matter of weeks. He gradually lost his novelty value, and so his eccentric behaviour was no longer a source of distraction. Stephen developed a bond with Martin and felt a strong duty of care towards him. He made every effort to ensure that the lad progressed at his own pace. The results were clear to see.

Martin made considerable progress in a very short period and became a much more contented young man. His parents acknowledged the contribution of his young teacher and even communicated their gratitude to the principal. Ordinarily, Stephen Daly's position would be enhanced by such favourable comments from a parent. Still, Stephen Daly's fate had already been sealed

The morning had gone badly, and he had only himself to blame. Stephen took advantage of his unusually long lunch break on a Monday to go back to the house for a little lie-down. He also felt able to take a bowl of soup and some bread. Drinking heavily on the eve of a school day was asking for trouble. It was difficult enough to manage the students at the best of times. To attempt to do so while nursing a hangover was bordering on the suicidal.

Stephen had not forgotten why he was sick today. The whiskey had failed to banish thoughts of Eva. He regretted his decision to stand her up. He wished that he could turn back the clock to Saturday afternoon. He also lamented that he had been so scared of the age difference between them. Furthermore, he wished that he were now with her.

Right now, she was probably at a working lunch with some building society manager. How wonderful would it be to be transported to her and tell her how much she meant to him?

He then thought of her mobile phone. He could talk to her now, but what would he say? What excuse could he possibly come up with that would repair the damage done?

At least he could be sure that she was not in her husband's company. To be doubly safe, he opted to use a public phone.

Having given himself a few moments to collect his thoughts, he decided to call her on her mobile. He planned to apologise for his standing her up. His excuse would be that his father was travelling to a conference in Donegal that evening, and he couldn't think of a good reason for not travelling with him.

He knew it wasn't a very plausible explanation, but all that was needed was an excuse to start the ball rolling again.
He keyed in the digits with unsure hands and waited, half expecting to hear her answering service. However, to his surprise, she immediately answered, instantly recognising her caller's voice.
There followed a moment of silence when both seemed afraid to speak. It was Eva who broke the embarrassing silence.
'Where have you been?'
Her tone displayed more puzzlement than true concern.
Stephen delivered his much-rehearsed lines.
'My Dad had to drive to a conference in Donegal. There was no way that I could refuse a lift to the door. I mean, how could I explain taking the train instead?'
'I see', Eva replied, unconvinced by the excuse but yet pleased that whatever rethink he might have been having was now apparently resolved in her favour.
Stephen breathed more freely. This was easier than he had imagined it would be.
'How come you are free now? Don't tell me that you are pulling a sickie on my poor Simon'.
He sought to reassure her
'No, it was nothing like that. I have a long dinner hour today. I'm calling you from the kiosk in Manor estate. Where are you now? Are you alone?'
'Yes, I am. I'm driving on the *M 50*. And it's free-flowing for a change. I have a couple of more calls to make before I head home.'

There was another prolonged silence. This time it was Stephen who took his courage into his hands.

'Can I see you soon?' he asked, trying to sound as a matter of fact as he could manage.

'I genuinely miss you,' he added.

He had not intended the latter remark. It just slipped out on him. There was no doubting the genuine feeling in his voice.

'I'm so glad that you feel like that', she breathed softly.

'But you can't call tonight. Simon will be at home all night, but tomorrow night he's gone from eight o'clock. There's yet another one of those meeting of Laity leaders tonight. They seem to have an awful lot to talk about recently, but who am I to complain?

'Keep your mobile close to you tomorrow evening. If there is any change in the plan, I'll call you. I have to go now, Stephen. Thanks for calling. It means a great deal to me'.

Knowing that he had not blown his chances with Eva, Stephen returned to school for the afternoon classes. There was a most discernible pep in his step. The hangover's symptoms had all but disappeared, but the lingering odour of stale beer was proving to be more stubborn.

As he was a few minutes early for a class, he decided on a quick cup of coffee in the staff room. Pamela was the only teacher present and appeared delighted to see him.

'And what was your weekend like, Stephen?'

'Nothing exciting! I was back in the bosom of the family. How are your parents, by the way, Pamela?'

'They're fine. Actually, Mum and Dad often mention you. You certainly created a good impression on them.'

Stephen smiled, graciously acknowledging the intended compliment.

'Yeah, I might give them a shout the next time I borrow the auld fella's car for a trip to Castlehome'.

Pamela nodded approval.

'That would be great'.

Pamela went on to say how much she was looking forward to the house party. It was certainly going to be a night to remember. Stephen assured her that he was counting the hours until then.

'We could all do with a bit of a party but remind me to go a bit easier on the bottle', he asked earnestly.

On Tuesday evening, Stephen's mobile phone remained silent. Simon Lynch was attending the meeting of the Laity Leaders in the Gateway Hotel. On the dot of eight-thirty, Stephen Daly was standing on the doorstep of the Lynch residence, a paper folder under his arm, still fearful of the possibility of prying eyes and wagging tongues.

Eva Lynch was waiting for his arrival. She opened the door invitingly before he even had an opportunity to reach for the bell.

Once inside, she pulled him close, holding him close to her.

'It's great to see you, Stephen.'

'Great to see you too! I missed you'.

Eva may have been pleased to see him, yet she seemed unconvinced as to his cover story.

'If you genuinely missed me, why was all the nonsense about conferences in Donegal? Why did you change your mind about seeing me again? Did you get cold feet?'

Eva was nothing if not direct. Her forthright approach caught him off guard. He immediately took on an embarrassed look before muttering something incoherent about his father passing through Castlehome.

'Funny time for a conference in Donegal, not exactly conference season, is it?

'By the way, what town was the conference in?'

'Ah, Bundoran, I think.'

'I wonder which hotel would have hosted that. I'll be travelling up there tomorrow. I might check with the receptionist. A conference of Local Authority executives, you said, wasn't it?'

Stephen was now under severe pressure.
'Maybe I'm wrong about Bundoran, but it was somewhere up there. It could have been Buncrana. What's the bloody difference anyway?'
Eva tapped him repeatedly on the chest with her accusing finger.
'The difference is more than sixty miles anyway', she answered before bluntly stating what she deduced from all this conference nonsense.
'You stood me up. And you dreamed up this daft excuse later, but am I complaining? You thought better of it, and here you are'.
There was little point in denying the truth of her assertion.
Stephen levelled with her as best he could but decided against telling her of his anxieties concerning her age.

Eva had half-expected to be stood up by this young man. There were bound to be conflicting pressures in his mind. She had been prepared for his retreat from her life. It would have hurt and disappointed her deeply, but such was the nature of relationships. She would not have been bitter. The truth was that she had privately vowed not to contact him or pressurise him in any way. A decision to meet her again had to come from him.
Now that the cross-questioning was over, she poured her guest a cup of coffee, earnestly requesting his honest opinion on its flavour. She planned to have some business associates around for a meal at the weekend. She intended to serve this new blend of coffee. It was a little strong for his taste.
'I will take that as a vote against.'
'What does he think about it?'

'Simon hasn't tasted it yet. Anyway, he's very predictable; I know he will like it.'

Stephen saw an opening here to explore some points, which had often exercised his mind.

'You have been together a long time now, haven't you?'

'Over fifteen years now! It's frightening to think how time passes', she mused before opening up to him as she had never done before.

'He was very nice to me back then. I had been through a hard time. Simon was there for me. *Solid as a rock*, as the song says. Simon was my rock.'

Stephen wondered where she and Simon had first met.

Eva thought for a moment, wondering perhaps how much she should say.

'I was working in Ennis while living at home in Limerick. He was attending some teachers' conference there. He came into the branch office to withdraw some money. We passed the time of day, and before I knew what had happened, I had agreed to go out for a meal with him. Looking back, I was probably on the rebound, but I felt secure and safe with him. The rest, as they say, is history.'

'You must have had the girls early on in the marriage'.

'You are not too slow. We had the twins very early in our relationship', she answered rather warily.

The coffee cups, once emptied, were immediately dispatched to the dishwasher. Eva raised herself onto his lap and asked about what was happening in his life. She was both amused and horrified by his account of being drunk at school. He thought it prudent to omit details of his wetting himself. It did not strike him as being in very good taste. Eva enquired about Sinead. For the first time, she confessed to being jealous of her.

'She's young and beautiful. You two can be seen together, and no one would raise an eyebrow. I envy her being free to be with you. You know what I mean. I wish you wouldn't go on seeing her', she added with the slightest hint of a tear forming in her eyes.

Stephen was more than a little surprised by this revelation. Certainly, he felt a strong attraction to Eva on a physical level. He also believed that his feelings went beyond the physical. He also had strong feelings for Sinead. Right now, he could compartmentalise his life. Sitting pretty in one mental compartment was Sinead, the girl for the social occasion, his girlfriend and prospective wife.

Eva was languishing seductively in another compartment, which was not as clearly labelled. She was his sometimes lover who could drive him to pitiful distraction with her captivating beauty and spellbinding sensuality. There was an aura of surrealism about her as if she were not for the real world.

'I don't know what you have to complain about,' he retorted.

'It's not as if Sinead and I are having it off together. She's not that type of girl'.

Before he had finished his sentence, he realised that he had left himself open for attack.

'And I am, then, so what does that make me? Some fallen woman or easy ride?'

'No', he replied earnestly but uncomfortably.
'I have genuinely fallen for you. One part of me shies away from you because you are a married woman, but how will I put this?
You are my true north. My compass always points to you. I find it very difficult not to follow it.'
Eva didn't know whether to be relieved or annoyed. She hung on his every word.
'I love being with you, Eva. What's more, I'm bloody miserable when I'm not. But I'll tell you this for nothing. At times, I'm afraid of you. But I haven't got my head around what exactly I feel for you.'
Stephen was now embarking on an impromptu assessment of their relationship, which even surprised him.
'I know where I stand with Sinead, for the moment anyway. She is my girlfriend, who incidentally is coming to Dublin with me on Saturday. She wants to do some Christmas shopping. As I was saying, I like her, but I crave you'.
It was strange, but in those few unrehearsed sentences, Stephen articulated his conflicting emotions more accurately than he could, with hours of rehearsal.

Out of the blue, Eva confessed that she and Simon had lived separate lives in recent times. She returned to explain an earlier remark that she had made.
'You asked whether my two girls must have come early in our marriage. Well, to be honest, they came too soon. I was three months pregnant when I walked up the aisle with Simon Lynch. I suppose I should say 'sprinted up the aisle,' she mused.

'Few knew anything on my wedding day, but they sure as hell knew soon after. And in case you're running away with any wrong ideas. Yes, he was the father. Even he never doubted that. Well, not to my face anyway,' she added, by way of an afterthought.
Stephen could not hide his disbelief.
'That's a surprise. I wouldn't have thought that old Simon believed in sex after marriage, much less sex before marriage'.
Eva heard but did not reply. She was still engrossed in her reveries.
'But my Simon did the honourable thing and married the woman he had so tarnished, as he saw it. I don't think we were ever really compatible. As well as that, he always believed that I had somehow ensnared him. He resented me for that. Life with him could be difficult enough at times, but thankfully there has been no problem recently.'

'Do you mean to say that Lynch would hit you?' Stephen asked in amazement.

Eva's eyes filled, and her hand trembled. She recounted traumatic details. The street angel and school saint could occasionally descend to a ferocious level. She sobbed as she described a series of black eyes and bruised ribs. There were never any broken bones, but the skin has been broken on several occasions. She rubbed off some makeup from around the eyes to reveal some scar tissue, testimony to a particularly severe beating some ten years previously. On that occasion, she required three stitches in the casualty department of the local hospital. She told the hospital staff that she had fallen from her bicycle, hitting against the iron railings outside the church.

'At least it made a change from walking into doors', supposed Stephen, his heart overflowing with sympathy.

'Did you never report him or leave him, or how on earth did it happen that he stopped at all?'

Eva moved away from him to hide the pain that was to be read in her reddening eyes.

'I never left him, nor did I make an official complaint', she recounted.

'It wasn't as if it was happening very frequently. There could be months between such violent outbursts. The problem was that you never knew what might provoke Simon.'

She related how she once had a confidential chat with the now-retired Sergeant Casey.

'He was of the old school, no-nonsense type guard. He had a quiet word in Simon's ear. He made it known, in no uncertain terms, what would happen if there were to be a recurrence. That was seven years ago. He has never raised a hand to me since. It humiliated him that anyone knew about it, especially the sergeant, who could use it against him one day'.

Stephen's face took on a more relieved aspect. However, he still had questions to ask.

'Did your daughters know anything about this, or did they ever witness violence?'

Eva shook her head while dabbing her moistened eyes with a tissue.

'No, thank God, they never witnessed anything untoward. I think that was just pure chance. He could be quite rough with them as well but never really violent. It was more a case of having no patience with them, constantly shouting at them, even physically pushing them out of his way.

The twins were beautiful girls who gave little or no trouble. That made no difference to him.'

Stephen was tempted to tell Eva that he too was a twin until his brother was killed, but he did not want to be seen to be trumping her trouble. This moment concerned Eva and her problems.

Eva was going with the flow in unburdening herself. She continued with her disclosures.

'When the twins finished primary school, I decided that they were going to boarding school, even though I would miss them enormously. Simon didn't like that decision. He didn't care about them but thought it might be perceived as a snub to the local schools, but I was insistent. Eventually, he relented. He knew that if he dug his heels in on the issue, I would leave him and take the twins. And there was no way that Simon Lynch would, in such circumstances, invite public ridicule. His image is so very important to him.'

These revelations were coming a little bit too hot and too heavy for Stephen. It was difficult for him to view so much dirty linen from the Lynch cupboard at once.

He had great difficulty reconciling the public persona of his principal with what he was now hearing.

He was interested in the thought process behind the boarding school decision.

'The girls were getting to a stage where they could detect an atmosphere and mood within the house. I feared that possibly they would have been forced into taking sides against him. It would spell the end of the happy family home for them. You see, when all is said and done, Simon is not all bad. At the back of it all, he probably loves those girls more than anything in the world, even though he may not show it very often. And more than likely, he loves me too. The first couple of years were incident-free, and I can honestly say that I was quite happy being married to him. He showed me love and kindness and would try to comfort me whenever I was down. For the last few years, he has been impeccable in his behaviour, but the bottom line is that we no longer live as man and wife, if you get my drift.'

Stephen had no difficulty with this, but he had trouble understanding why she had stayed with him all those years.

Eva answered as honestly as she could.

'The children, the security, the fear of being alone, the stigma, But, I suppose, Stephen, there are many reasons for staying. There is always the fear that you may be jumping from the frying pan into the fire.'

'But surely, a woman like you would have very little difficulty in starting with someone else', he said. 'From what you told me, there were probably grounds for an annulment in your case. A neighbour of ours in Dublin got one of those. Did you ever check that out?'

'I considered everything, but I did nothing. The only drastic action I took was to ensure that we had no more children. I went on the pill at the first available opportunity. Later I had myself sterilised'.

Stephen shook his head, acknowledging that this disclosure answered an unasked question of his own. He could not understand why any man, on the wrong side of forty at the time of marriage, should be resentful about marrying a clever and beautiful woman with a pleasing personality.

What had started very much as a night of unconfined passion had somehow turned into something much deeper that had drawn them closer. Going home that night, Stephen felt that his relationship with Eva had ascended to a higher and potentially more dangerous level.

.

Owing to a combination of factors, Eva and Stephen did not meet up for the remainder of the week. On Saturday, she was home again with Simon. In addition, Simon was due to attend a conference in Limerick over the weekend. However, because of Stephen's trip to Dublin with Sinead, they were obliged to disregard a perfect opportunity to get together. Stephen lost interest in the shopping trip. Sinead was a very special girl. However, the new reality was that Eva had usurped her place in his thoughts.

He took Sinead to the family home in Castleknock in time for Saturday lunch. On Saturdays, dinner was later in the evening. Breakfast tended to be a protracted business on a Saturday morning as the entire family was on a day off.

Stephen's father, Frank, generally fitted in a round of golf before lunch. His mother was busy in the kitchen when her son and his girlfriend called.

Stephen noted with pleasure that Sinead seemed quite at home, chatting amiably with his mother.

'Stephen tells me that you were an air hostess. That must have been a very exciting career.'

'Oh yes, I suppose, there was the novelty element at the start. I enjoyed foreign travel and meeting different people. Stephen's dad and I got many a cheap trip abroad. The job was considered glamorous, but like many glamorous jobs, it quickly became routine.'

Sinead was genuinely interested, as she had once considered that same career path.

'When I left school, I toyed with the idea of becoming an air hostess. I got information leaflets from the Career Guidance teacher, but nursing was always my first love'.

Rosaleen Daly smilingly nodded her approval of that decision.

'Nursing is a career for life. The job of air hostess suits younger, single people. It is very difficult when you have young children and have to be away from them'.

The turning of a key in the door signalled the return of Stephen's father. Frank Daly's imposing frame filled the doorway. He stood well over six feet tall and was built to match. He gave his son a welcoming slap on the back. He then approached his son's girlfriend and extended a welcoming hand to her.

His wife, Rosaleen, could tell by the colour of Frank's complexion that he had been drinking. He liked to enjoy a couple of pints when one of his mates was driving. Ordinarily, he was of a reserved nature, but he became more chatty and gregarious with a little alcohol in him.

'You're very welcome, Sinead. I'm sorry to hear that you have been saddled with this scoundrel. And you seem to be such a nice girl.'

'Ah, he's not the worst. Did you enjoy your game of golf, Mr Daly?'

'I did indeed love, and by the way, call me Frank; Frank by name and frank by nature.'

'How did you play today?' asked Rosaleen.

'I played pretty well. Well enough, anyway, to take a fiver off the boys', he said, still basking in the minor glory of it.
'Golf is a great game. Did you ever consider taking up the game yourself, Sinead?'
'Not really, but maybe later on. My father is a golfer, but I could never see its appeal.'
'I know what you mean, a good walk spoiled. I came to golf late in life. I was more a hurling man, you know, being from Tipperary, but when you're getting on a bit, golf is the only game.'
The mention of Tipperary reminded him of his son's colleague.
'By the way, Stephen, that Corrigan teacher you mentioned, did you ever ask him if he was anything to Martin Corrigan from Cashel?'

'I asked him. Martin is his first cousin. He told Martin that you were asking for him. The poor man is in a bad way with arthritis now. He's on a waiting list for a hip replacement.'
Frank was sorry to hear that. Rosaleen was more interested in discovering how Sinead and her son had met.
Sinead beat Stephen to the answer.
'A mutual friend introduced us'.
'That mutual friend has a lot to answer for', Frank jokingly commented.
'I see dear, that you stopped off at the 19th hole for a little aperitif', his wife said.
'Yea, I had a couple of pints, but where was I just now?'
Stephen's dad politely enquired how his guest was enjoying her nursing career.
She assured him that she liked the job despite the occasional bad days.

Frank believed that nurses were unusual in public sector employment in that those in the private sector viewed them favourably.

'Local government administrators, like me, are dismissed as pencil pushers. We are nearly seen as being spongers on the exchequer payroll. And it's even worse for teachers like Stephen here. I used to tell him to forget about teaching and train in Information Technology or Law instead. He would have more pay and less aggravation'.

'Maybe I should have listened to you', confided Stephen.

Stephen's mother was genuinely concerned.

'Is it that bad, Stephen? Surely, you are exaggerating'.

It was an ideal opportunity to prepare her for what would inevitably follow. His fate was out of his own hands now. Considering the principal and the parents' negative attitude towards him, it was unlikely that his contract would be extended beyond the end of the school year.

Stephen was now in full flow on the subject.

'It is that bad. Sometimes, it is even worse than bad. It is not so much teaching as crowd control. A lot of lads have no interest in learning anything. It certainly looks easier from the outside.'

His father listened attentively and was disappointed at what he was hearing.

'There is no respect anymore. People are encouraged to be familiar with their rights but not with their responsibilities. In my day, it was very different.'

Rosaleen was keen to interrupt her husband lest he monopolised the conversation.

'Right, Frank, Sinead isn't interested in Ancient History.'

Lorraine and Niamh soon joined the table for lunch. The girls were in lively giggling form, kicking their big brother under the table and laughing at their private little jokes. They told Sinead that Stephen had promised to take them down to Castlehome for a weekend. It all seemed so exciting for two young, fun-loving teenagers.
Sinead was delighted. She insisted that they let her know well in advance so that she could arrange time off. She even offered them accommodation in her house.
Lorraine was anxious to stay with her brother for a rather unlikely reason.
'Thank you, but we want to stay in Stephen's house. We've heard so much about Tom Clarke and his singing.'
It was abundantly clear to all present that it was not Tom's singing alone that stimulated this desire to meet him. It was more his single status than his singing status that interested them.
'Tom seems to be popular with the ladies. Is that true, Sinead?' Rosaleen enquired.
'Yea, Tom is certainly entertaining. He is also very nice but not as nice as your son.'
Niamh was interested in nursing as a career. She had many questions for Sinead. She was keen to learn what the job entailed and especially what it was like to work through the night. Niamh graciously accepted an invitation to a guided tour of Castlehome hospital whenever the proposed trip materialised.
After lunch, Sinead and Stephen went into town accompanied by his two sisters. She enjoyed the company of his sisters. A welcome bonus

for Sinead was the sisters' willingness to offer opinions and advice on the clothes she was trying on.

Sinead knew that Stephen was not one for waiting around women's clothes shops. She suggested that he go off on his own for a couple of hours and meet up with them later. They arranged to meet up inside the main door of *Eason* in O' Connell Street.

Stephen bought a newspaper and settled down with a *Club Rock Shandy* in a city-centre pub. He hoped to enjoy a quiet read of the paper and catch the soccer scores on the television.

Inevitably, his thoughts turned to Eva Lynch, all alone in that house in Castlehome. He would love to be with her right now. As he could not be with her, he decided to give her a call.

She had been in town doing the weekly shopping and was just in the door. She was looking forward to a relaxing evening in front of the television.

'It is not what I hoped for. Anyway, I will make the best of it.'

Stephen apologised, assuring her that he would prefer to be with her than killing time around Dublin city centre.

Not surprisingly, Stephen was first at Eason's bookstore. Sinead and the girls had a busy couple of hours. The number of carrier bags certainly bore testimony to some productive shopping. Sinead was particularly pleased with a new top and trousers that she had purchased.

I will try it on for you when we get back.'

She intended to wear it at the party on Friday evening. There was nothing like a spot of retail therapy to lift a woman's spirits.

Over dinner, Frank had a pleasant surprise in store for his son.
'A young man in your position needs a car. I am going to lend you the price of a good second-hand model. When you get back down the country, shop around for one about three or four years old.'
Stephen could not believe his luck. This weekend had not been a total write off, after all.
'Buy from a reputable dealer, not from some chancer advertising in the local paper', he warned.
Stephen assured him that he would follow his advice.
'I won't charge you any interest. You can pay me back a certain amount every month. What do you say to that?'
'Wow, I'd say,' grinned an excited young man.
'Thanks a million! I'll set up a direct debit'.

For the rest of the evening, Stephen was like a kid looking forward to Santa Claus.
He speculated on what make of car he might be available. The colour might be important too. Ideally, he would love a sunroof, sports wheels and rear spoilers. Nevertheless, he intended to be sensible and go for value for money over style.
Rosaleen Daly showed Sinead her room for the night. She did not care what the couple might get up to in Castlehome. In her house, she called the shots. She had been delighted to welcome Sinead, but there would be no sleeping together under her roof.
Frank Daly dropped the young couple at the railway station in time for the Sunday evening train. True to form, the train developed an engine problem. On this occasion, it occurred just outside Mullingar. The

passengers had to wait for a fleet of buses to take them on the remainder of their journey. Because of the location, they had to climb a ladder onto the embankment to reach those busses.
'Maybe, we should stay over in Pamela's homeplace', Stephen joked.
'In your dreams!'
It had been a nightmarish trip. The buses eventually reached Castlehome at ten minutes past eleven, two hours behind schedule. Despite the frustration and fatigue, Stephen gratefully looked on the bright side. It would be the last time that he would be at the mercy of this railway line. Next time he would have his own transport.

The dark and dreary days of winter are tolerable only because we cling steadfastly to the expectation of better days to come. These are the dark hours before the dawn, the short days before the long.
As soon as school finished, it was nearly lighting up time. The country was almost immediately pitched into depressing darkness. There was little or no incentive to take to the great outdoors, to inhale the cold and refreshing air of winter or to shake off the seasonal feeling of lethargy and sloth.
Castlehome was like an animal in hibernation. It had shut down for the winter in all but its basic functioning. Unfortunately, the same could not be said for Saint Jude's.

The arrival of the first of the winter snow seemed to propel their already high spirits onto an even higher orbit.
It was as if the snow contained some behaviour-modifying ingredient, which made almost the entire student population regress to an even more juvenile mental state. Maybe it was the purity of its form, which, on an unconscious level, reminded them of a more innocent past. More likely, it was merely that this snow provided them with another potent weapon in their relentless rebellion against discipline and authority.
Even in the darkest of moments, a chink of light can offer a degree of hope or comfort. Not every one of Stephen Daly's classes was an occasion for student insurrection and defiance. In many of his classes, work proceeded with admirable pace and competence. The trouble for Stephen was that the gross misbehaviour of the few tarnished his reputation in the eyes of management and parents. It also served to undermine his fragile confidence and make him question his career

choice. If that bare arse had not appeared at the door on his first day, there was no telling how different his story might have been.

In a school situation, trouble begets trouble, and it becomes a vicious circle, which is virtually impossible to break. Much of the misbehaviour in Stephen's classroom came from well adjusted but opportunistic students. They seized the prospect of having their fun with a raw recruit and were confident that they could act with impunity. Their story was that that teacher was inexperienced and vulnerable, and they shamelessly exploited this. For others, serious background issues in their individual lives could explain the story behind their misbehaviour. More often than not, these individuals were more to be pitied than punished. Of course, most students were well behaved and conscientious. Yet, it only takes one or two in each class to disrupt the learning process.

While Stephen was attempting to introduce his Fourth Year class to the wonder of Yeats's poetry, a counter-attraction proved difficult to compete with. Their attention had been hijacked by a fall of white, powdery snow.

It was one additional challenge for the young teacher.

He was reaching the end of his tether with them. He could not resist the temptation to be nasty.

'I usually have to cope with just one shower, but today I have to cope with two'.

James Reidy was the first to get the insult.

'That's not nice, Sir. My dad will not like that. He already thinks that you're not fit to be a teacher. He saw you in Taylor's lately. You were ossified. You were puking into the wash-hand basin.'

Moans of disgust came from all four corners of the room.

Young Reidy was enjoying his moment in the spotlight.

A particularly forthright lad at the back of the class broadened out the discussion. He related how one particular Christmas Day, his father, heavy from the weight of drink, got sick onto their turkey.

'I remember that the stuffing was a bit sour that Christmas'.

Stephen had only himself to blame. He had provoked the comment by his injudicious remark.

Before starting the selected poems on the course, Stephen delivered a short outline of Yeats's main influences. This was intended to whet the appetite and to put his work into some perspective. His introduction touched on the poet's infatuation with Maud Gonne. Such things certainly grabbed their attention, not because of any sensibility on their part to the misery of unrequited love. Rather it seemed to hold out the prospect of a discussion on sex.

The questions came thick and fast.

'Did they get it on together?'

'Would she be as sexy as Jordan, the Page 3 model?'

Stephen asked the boys to open their books while they read the first poem.

There was the inevitable reaction.

'Will we be taking notes today? My pen's robbed'.

'I don't have a book! Hey, Sir, get them to lend me a book. They have two books at their desk'.

The response from that desk was belligerently negative.

'Buy your own fucking books'.

Such a reaction was interpreted as a personal insult, which must be met in kind.

'Go away, Clarke, your father is a wanker, and what's more, your mother is as ugly as sin. She shaves more often than your father does'.

Whatever about their fathers, the boys were particularly sensitive to comments about their respective mothers.

Stephen had to re-assert himself.

'There will be no derogatory language in my classroom. If you don't behave, you'll have to leave.'

By now on his feet, Clarke was ready to fight to defend his mother's honour if not her countenance.

It looked ominously like a fistfight was going to develop. The teacher had to re-establish order.

'For the last time, I'm telling you both to sit down, or I will throw both of you out.'

'You and whose army?' growled Clarke, still incensed at the unmannerly reference to his mother. Stephen could see that he had lost any semblance of control in the classroom. The reality was that the room would probably have been quieter if he had not been there at all. His professional career lay in tatters all around him. It was a painful realisation for him.

'Yea, you throw us out, is it? That's a laugh. Soon, there'll be no one left in this class at all.'

What could he do? The boys were right.

The exodus started as a dribble before growing into a flood. Over half the parents had their sons moved out of his class. He was left with the children of the less interested or perhaps less well-informed parents. Lynch constantly lectured him on the need to impose himself and to take charge, yet he never explained how this might be accomplished.

When the class had settled to an acceptable level of rowdiness, he resumed his discussion on the selected poem.

Reidy fancied himself as the comedian.

'Sir, we had a dog called Maud.'

For the next twenty minutes, Stephen painstakingly took the class through the poem's thought sequence. All was going well until the boys were distracted again.

A snowball fight in the yard had grabbed their attention. There followed a predictable rush to the window. With blatant disregard for Stephen's orders, they opened the classroom window. Every conceivable insult was hurled at the group below them.

'Go on, Kelly, you stupid prick!'

'Casey, you can't even throw a snowball straight. You couldn't hit a bank of turf.'

Further derogatory comments rained down on the now vengeful group. Then, in a moment, there was a sudden retreat from the window. A fist full of snow flew across the room. One young boy, who was a bit too slow to take evasive action, had suffered a direct hit in his left eye. 'Bullseye'! Reidy shouted with glee.

Things could hardly sink lower, or could they?' Sometimes there is no more dangerous opponent than a man who has nothing left to lose. Stephen now found himself in that category.

Belatedly, he sprung into action. He slammed down the window but not before he had been showered with melting snow. The young student was holding his hand to his eye but yet issuing blood-curdling threats to the perpetrator.

To discover the extent or the nature of the injury, Stephen pulled the victim's hand away from the affected eye. The eye was already badly swollen. Under college rules, any such incident must be reported to management and the relevant details logged. One could not be too careful when litigation was a possibility.

At the end of class, he left the room to take the victim to the principal's office. Along the way, he stopped to consult with Jimmy Corrigan. He had seen and recognised the boys who had thrown the snowballs. He would give their names to the principal.

Stephen left his friend and took the much-travelled path to the principal, knowing full well the reception he was likely to receive. It certainly looked as if Stephen's days in St. Jude's were numbered.

Eva Lynch warned Stephen that Simon had changed his mind about going out. Stephen was not to come to the house. Instead, he was to meet her at a secluded spot, just off the Dublin Road. It was risky, but at this stage, Stephen was prepared to take risks. Eva's excuse for her husband was that she was visiting her friend Marjorie.

There was no question but that Stephen was getting deeper and deeper into this relationship. Conversely, his relationship with Sinead had been relegated to the back burner.

Sinead was conscious of a definite change in their relationship. On several recent occasions, she had complained about his seeming lack of attention. She questioned him as to whether he still had feelings for her.

Stephen could honestly put his hand on his heart and swear that his love for her was undiminished, but that would be being disingenuous. While his feelings for Sinead largely remained the same, the reality was that Stephen was now head over heels in love with Eva. He could not envisage his future without her. But what was he to do about Sinead?

He still loved Sinead but in a different way. There was less of the passion and more of the friendship, which in itself would seem to augur better for an enduring relationship. There were no complications with Sinead. He could marry her in the morning and live a very happy life had it not been for Eva. Eva was to him what the prospect of the jackpot is to a gambler. It made him risk the proverbial bird in the hand, but he could well end up losing both.

All this cloak and dagger business initially excited Stephen. It caused his adrenaline to rush and gave him a feeling of enormous excitement and a confirmation of the fact that he was truly alive. Recently it had become tedious and bothersome.

He hated all the sneaking around. It made him feel less of a man and more of the pathetic wimp he sometimes feared he was in danger of becoming.

But then, in Eva's presence, she made him feel like a red-blooded man again.

However, decisions had to be made. These would be hard decisions, and they would soon have to be made.

On the night before the party, Stephen was feeling distinctly unsociable. An abscess on a tooth was causing him great pain. The dentist had prescribed a course of antibiotics. As a consequence, alcohol was not recommended for the duration of that course of treatment.

Stephen was not one of those happy souls who could have as much fun sober. With him, there had always been some little reserve or inhibition that alcohol overcame. He was not looking forward to the party, but he felt obliged to put in an appearance.

For others, it would be a night of celebration. The school term was nearing its end, and the prospect of two weeks holidays had raised many spirits. When the idea of a party had first been mooted, Stephen had imagined that it would be a night of celebration for him too. However, in the interim, life had become much more complicated for him. It was now time for him to have the courage of his convictions.

He must put one of the women out of her misery. It was now time to be brave and decisive.

On Friday, December 12, the party was in full swing when Stephen and Tom arrived at ten o'clock. It was early in the night for a full house as people generally waited until the pubs closed to attend a house party. The living room and kitchen of No.22 had been festooned with bunting and streamers. Multicoloured balloons of every shape and size adorned the ceiling and wall tops. Some romantic spirit had strategically positioned mistletoe over the hall door. Whether this was an attempt to lay claim to an unsuspecting guest on arrival or a last desperate snog at the end of the night, it was impossible to say.

Ordinarily, there were a few here that Stephen would not mind getting under the mistletoe with, toothache or no toothache. Some of these hitherto unseen beauties were nurses from the hospital, invited by Sinead and Susan. There were also some girls from the Asset Management section of the bank.

'I wouldn't mind letting them handle my assets', whispered Tom.

'I'd say they'd see strong growth even in the very short term', he laughed.

Stephen smiled, but his mind was not on Tom's double entendre.

Two girls approached the two lads. They had recognised the two lads from Taylor's pub.

'Hi, I'm Wendy, and this is my friend Sandra. I feel as if I know you, Tom, from playing in the pub. I really like your singing'.

Stephen could not resist making fun of Tom.

'Now Tom, didn't I tell you, if you waited long enough, there was bound to be someone who liked it? Maybe these could be your very first groupies'.

Wendy turned her attention to Stephen.

'You work with Tom, don't you?'

Stephen realised just how small the town was.

'You teach a brother of mine in St. Jude's. He enjoys your classes', she said. It was nice to be complimented, or so he thought.

'I like to make learning fun. I'm glad that your brother finds my class enjoyable. What's your brother's name?'

Wendy took a sip from her glass before she answered.

'James is his name. James Reidy. He's in Fourth Year'.

Seldom had a girl lost her appeal so suddenly.

He did not want to be in her company for a second longer. Even though she had done nothing wrong, it was a form of guilt by association. Only a few hours earlier, he had caught her brother attempting to melt the classroom globe with a cigarette lighter. Global warming had suddenly become a burning issue in Castlehome.

Stephen excused himself and went to grab a word with Sinead. She was busy passing around trays of savouries.

'I see you have met the shy and retiring Wendy. You might be interested to know that she is footloose and fancy-free again. Her boyfriend left her for a girl in the bacon factory.'

Stephen had no difficulty in understanding this.

'I'm not surprised. I'd have left her, too, even for bloody Ellen Hayes'.

'Just make sure you are not caught under the mistletoe with her', she added with a mischievous wink.

Stephen was determined that such a scenario would not happen.

'I wouldn't be caught under the same sky as her or that waster of a brother.'
Stephen's stabbing pain in his back tooth struck again with a savage vengeance. He passed much of the night bent over the kitchen sink, gargling with whiskey. Some person mentioned that spirits might dull the pain.
While he was gargling, Pamela approached, concern etched on her face.
'What are you doing? Are you feeling alright?'

As Tom went off to mingle, Stephen explained about the abscess on the tooth. She was most sympathetic and advised him to go home and even hinted that she was willing to be his ministering angel. Stephen was inclined to take her advice but passed on her dubious offer of companionship. God only knows what interpretation she would put on that for her housemate, Sinead.
The party was shaping up to be a really enjoyable one. There was more than a generous supply of food and drink. There was also a lovely seasonal atmosphere. Cupid was busy too, as newly introduced couples smooched as they closely swayed to the timeless love songs' gentle rhythms.
As Stephen told Sinead of his intention to retire for the night, Tom came from behind him and planted a soft kiss on Sinead's lips.
'That's what you get, Sinead, if you insist on standing under the mistletoe'.
Stephen looked up, unperturbed.

'Sinead, I'd better step aside here and head home before this sex maniac jumps on me too. That is all I'd need tonight.'

When Stephen left the house, he double-checked to make sure that he was not being followed. Safely home, he turned on the lights and threw himself into a comfortable armchair. He decided to boil up the kettle and have a quick mug of tea before climbing the stairs to bed.
The stench of sour milk and the sight of unwashed dishes met him as he entered the kitchen. As he waited for the kettle to boil, he searched for the cleanest dirty mug, before rinsing it under the cold tap. He fished out a few teaspoons and similarly rinsed them in cold water. The hot tea had a surprisingly soothing effect on his painful mouth. He was now more inclined to sit back and scan the sport's pages of the evening paper.

Five minutes later, the doorbell rang. Stephen debated whether he should answer it or not. If it were Pamela, the door would remain locked to her. He crept to the darkened living room, from where he could get a side view of the front door from behind the curtains. Recognising the distinctive figure of Pamela Mc Enroe, he was glad that he exercised some caution.
Pamela was looking up, her eyes focused on the upstairs window. She was checking whether he had retired for the night. There was no way that he was going to open that front door. The last thing he wanted right now was a dose of Pamela Mc Enroe. The bell rang once, it rang twice, and it rang three times. Then, it stopped. There was no sound for about two minutes. Stephen felt that he could breathe again. He tiptoed to the room window to check that she had departed. Feeling a bit more confident, he drew the curtain aside. He jumped with fright so much

that he thought his heart would burst. He found himself staring into the monstrous visage that was pressed right up to the window.

There, looking in at him, with her hands up against the glass, was the would-be ministering angel. She signalled to Stephen to open the front door. His mind was working overtime to come up with a reason to explain his behaviour.

Pamela looked at him in disbelief.

'Stephen, I have been standing out there ringing that bell for the last five minutes.'

'Oh, Pamela, I'm sorry. Tom told me this evening that the bell is out of order. We must get someone to look at it. I thought I heard something outside, so I was taking a look.'

'Anyway, I'm in now. I hope you have the heat on because I'm freezing', She added, cupping her hands together.

Stephen did his best to appear tired and sore.

'I was going to the bedroom and was just looking around for my slippers.'

'I didn't know you were a slippers man', she said, glad that she had gleaned a little personal detail, which might complete her mental jigsaw of Stephen Daly.

He didn't wear bedroom slippers. It was the first thing that came into his mind, but now that he had mentioned them, he had to run with it.

'Oh, yes! I'm a real slippers man.'

Pamela seemed to approve of this settled form of domesticity and possibly imagined herself in years to come sharing this nightly routine.

A moment later and Stephen was mortally embarrassed. There was another ringing of the doorbell. It was loud and reverberated all around the house. Only the stone deaf could miss it.

'It must have come unstuck', Stephen said, desperately trying to save face.

He answered the door. Tom stood on the doorstep. He had come back as he had forgotten his guitar.

'I was hoping that you weren't in bed. I seem to have mislaid my key'.

Stephen pulled Tom aside. He threatened all kinds of lasting damage to his youthful body if he did not immediately haul Pamela back to the party with him. In fairness to Tom, he obliged, citing both Stephen's lamentable condition and the prospect of a party that was just taking off.

Left alone again, Stephen heaved a massive sigh of relief. He was not one for duplicity, and he certainly felt nothing but discomfort at the thought of Pamela Mc Enroe. In theory, being pursued by an eligible female was very flattering. However, when there was neither chemistry nor genuine friendship between them, it all became rather tedious.

At least at the party, she might find some man who might suit her. He considered it unlikely that she would meet anyone from the warm slippers and milk brigade.

Sometimes when one feels pushed in a certain direction, the natural inclination is to lean the opposite way. There was an obstinate streak in Stephen. Whether it was advisable or not, he was now more determined than ever to hang in at St. Jude's in an attempt to turn his fortunes around. No fifteen-year-old brats were going to undermine the course of his professional life. Neither was the wife-beater, Simon Lynch going to intimidate him. If he were to leave St. Jude's, he would be doing so on his own terms and in his own time. He would show Lynch and show the world that he was a force to be reckoned with.

This was the old Stephen Daly speaking. Not since the start of September had he heard himself utter these words. Only for that bare-arse brat, things could have been so different. It was incredible the little things that mark the difference between success and failure in the classroom. Still, one had to play the hand that one had been dealt. His was surely the original bum deal.

That day in the office, after the snowball incident, had been a turning point for him. Lynch had been most scathing and condescending in his pronouncements on Stephen.

'Damn it, lad, but you should have at least kept them away from the windows. It's not as if you have a big class to control. How is this going to read in the papers if it should ever go to court?

What sort of school will people think I'm running here? You're young and inexperienced but surely to God, you can at the very least keep them from sticking their heads out the open windows.'

Lynch seemed especially angry with Stephen. He did not mince his words.

'You need to watch your step outside of school too. Now, you might well say that that has no bearing on your job here. However, it has a bearing on it. If you are out drinking and carrying on at night, you are in no fit condition to take a class.'

Despite the tension between Lynch and himself, Stephen took his criticisms very much to heart. He could see that Lynch's complaints were fair and well-founded. He accepted that his performance had left much to be desired. Nevertheless, he was working at being a good teacher despite his rather unhelpful extra-curricular activities. He now strove to make classes as interesting as he possibly could.

He had organised the showing of what he considered to be interesting and yet relevant videos. No matter what topic he was teaching, there would be interesting anecdotes. Whenever possible, he introduced humour. That was one aspect of the modern teacher's role, which Lynch had undervalued. Young people of the age group represented at St. Jude's have a remarkably low boredom threshold.

Stephen reflected that he would not have gone into the teaching profession had he wished to become an entertainer. He would have chosen a less stressful job. Thinking back to his lectures on *Classroom Management*, he realised how totally ineffective the guidelines had been. There had been little of real value in those particular lectures at all. The impression conveyed was that a potentially troublesome student could be discouraged by a stern look from the apprentice teacher or by a targeted movement in his direction.

This notion of proximity control was about as useful as wagging a finger at a charging bull. The textbooks on teaching practice were not written by practising teachers in more unruly schools. He decided that a stricter approach was called for and would start immediately after the Christmas holidays.

For the moment, Stephen's mind was on his new car, which was ready for collection. He would have it for the trip home. The vehicle he finally settled on was a three-year-old *Volkswagen Golf*. The car came taxed for three months. Of course, the insurance premium had to be paid. Stephen was on the wrong side of twenty-five when it came to motor insurance costs. However, he had been, for some years, a named driver on his father's policy.

When the car arrived, Stephen was as excited as any new mother bringing her baby home for the first time. Even though it was not dirty, he still took it to the automatic car wash at the filling station. The tyre pressure was checked, as was the oil level. Everything was in order.

The honour of being the first passenger in his new car was bestowed on Sinead. On its maiden voyage, they drove to the village of Ardbane, where they stopped for a cup of coffee at the Village Inn. A roaring fire was in place to welcome the visitors from Castlehome. Considering the time of year, they ordered hot whiskeys. It was more a case of the power of suggestion, as at least four of the clientele were already enjoying the warm tipple. At any rate, it was the motoring equivalent of wetting the baby's head.

Stephen considered Sinead to be particularly quiet. She seemed preoccupied with some situation or other. She looked like one there on sufferance or possibly, she had something important to impart to him. He knew that he had annoyed her by cancelling several arrangements to meet her recently. The reality was that his meetings with Eva were, by their nature, hastily arranged and dependent on her husband's movements.

Stephen was not at all looking forward to Christmas. Certainly, it was great to get a break from the madhouse that was St Jude's, but Christmas brought unwelcome complications. Eva's twins, Melanie and Katie, would be home from boarding school for the holiday period. Eva had arranged to take some of her annual holidays to be with them. That was great for her but not such good news for him. However, she had agreed to meet him in Dublin early in the New Year before school resumed. They would have a full day together, a great improvement on a few snatched moments they recently enjoyed.

Sinead was scheduled for work on Christmas Day. After that, she intended to head south to Tralee to spend a few days with her family. Stephen was invited along, but he politely declined the invitation. He insinuated that he would make the trip early in the New Year.

Tom Clarke was only spending a couple of days with his family. He had been booked to play in Taylor's bar over the festive period. Christmas would bring the crowds back to the town for a week or so. It was also a good time of year to meet a new woman, perhaps someone from the area, who had come home for the holidays. Tom felt confident that romance might blossom for him in mid-winter. He had his eye on one girl in particular. At least, that is what he told Stephen. No doubt, Tom would play his cards close to his chest.

As for Stephen, he would ring in the New Year in the warm embrace of his family in Castleknock. A new year held out the promise of better times and provided an occasion for people to consider fresh starts. In that spirit, the Daly family travelled into Dublin City Centre for the New Year celebrations. The fireworks were nothing short of spectacular. There was a wonderful feeling of goodwill and optimism. Stephen saw the New Year as drawing a very definite line under past heartache. 1998 seemed to offer promise, even if that promise was tempered by concern surrounding the recent complexities in his life. He wished that things could be more simple and choices more clear. He was determined to use 1998 as an opportunity to get his life back on track.

On January 4, Eva met Stephen at a city-centre car park. Eva, cognisant of the risk of being recognised in the capital, took some precautions. She greeted her young man discreetly, with a tender display of affection that would not be out of place between mere acquaintances during the festive period. They walked side by side to the lifts of the multi-storey park and made their way through the thronged streets, where swarms of bargain hunters braved the bitter frosty air of early January.

Eva had her shopping list. She browsed through what seemed an endless succession of stores to get the right shade of purple in a sweater for Melanie. She also purchased a pair of stylish shoes in Size 4 for Katie. There was even something for Simon. Eva picked up a smart navy blazer for him with matching grey pants.

'It certainly will make a change from those bloody awful tweeds', commented Stephen.

Eva smiled knowingly.

'You wouldn't believe all the smart jackets and suits that that man has in his wardrobe, but it has to be the tweeds for school for some reason. He must see it as a sort of uniform. God, you'd swear he hadn't a stitch. People must think that I spend all our clothing allowance on myself', she chuckled.

For herself, she bought a beautifully tailored business suit. Stephen's patience was rewarded with a designer label sport's shirt. That shirt cost more than he would pay for his accommodation in a month. He would make a point of wearing it to their next meeting.

When she had completed the shopping, they returned to the car park to deposit Eva's purchases in her car boot. Stephen tossed the package containing his newly acquired attire in the boot of the *VW Golf*. Leaving Eva's car in the parking area, they both sat into the Golf to head out of town. There was less likelihood of being recognised outside of the city's shopping streets.

He drove Eva southbound in the direction of Wicklow. All the while, they chatted incessantly. An opportunity for such a heart to heart was unlikely to present itself again in the short term. En route, they came across a quaint old public house up in the foothills of the Wicklow Mountains. Despite it being into January, the bar still offered complimentary mulled wine.

Relaxing in front of the open turf fire, Eva unashamedly announced that she was thrilled to see him again. He had already guessed as much. For the duration of the journey, she had her hand resting on his left knee. It was as if she needed reassurance of his continued presence. Eva had become accustomed to brief moments of intense and exciting pleasure while they were together. Unfortunately, these had been invariably followed by longer periods of depression and frustration when he would take his leave of her.

Stephen experienced similar feelings. When he was in her presence, life was always wonderful and exciting. Whenever they were apart, life took on a more jaundiced aspect. Eva was now, very definitely the light of his world and this radiant creature, alongside him, brightened up this winter's day in a way no sun could ever manage.

Eva's children were home from boarding school. She was delighted to have them with her again. The trouble was that this coincided with Simon being especially short-tempered and disagreeable. He had disappeared on the Friday before Christmas without saying where he was going or whom he was meeting. In the past, that sort of behaviour was unknown to her. Recently it had become the norm.

'Maybe he's going through the male menopause ', Stephen remarked.

'I don't know what he's going through, but I hope he comes out the other end pretty quickly. I suspect that he's beginning to suffer a bit from depression. He goes off on his own more than he ever did. He never bothers with friends anymore. Peter Jennings, the bank manager, asked me recently why he had given up on the Laity Leaders. I thought he was still an active member. I recall that he recently told me only a while back that he was going to one of their meetings. That was one of the nights on which you called over'.

Stephen was equally mystified. He wondered why she had not directly questioned him on this.

'Do you know, I really don't care anymore. Anyway, I know where Simon was for some of the nights. Gerry Boyle saw him driving into the school a couple of evenings at nine o'clock or so. Hasn't he little to interest himself', she asked with disbelief.

'Wouldn't you think that he would see enough of that place during the day?'

Stephen could not understand that sort of behaviour at all.

'If I were married to the likes of you, I'd be at home every night with you making mad passionate love to you in front of the open fire'.

The novelty can wear off very quickly', Eva remarked.
Stephen acted as if he hadn't even heard her comment.
'And only when we'd be utterly drained we would climb the stairs to bed. There would be no time for paperwork. Fuck school! I say. Fuck everything to do with school'.
Eva smiled as she attempted to envisage that particular scenario.
'Stephen, do you think that we can ever be together, I mean together, or are we just fooling ourselves?'
'I certainly hope that we can be', he instantly replied.
This was something he had considered.
'It all depends on how much we want it to happen. I had a lot of time for thinking over Christmas. I have managed to get a lot of things clear in my mind. I can guarantee you that 1998 will see a new Stephen Daly'.
Eva was not convinced that there had been any need for a change.
'Well, I quite liked the old one. Please don't leave me in suspense, Stephen. Tell me, what changes can I expect to see in you?'
Stephen spoke in very measured tones as she hung on his every word.

'For a start, I am convinced that you are the woman for me. You are the only one I really and truly care about to the extent that I would risk everything for you'.
That was a big statement from him. He paused to gauge the impact of his words on the woman concerned.
To him, her expression was inscrutable, so he continued with his answer.

'I probably need my head examined with all the frustration and hassle that goes along with seeing you'.

Eva began to show a response. Initially, she had been caught wrong-footed by this disclosure. Now, she seemed pleased. There still remained a fly in the ointment.

'And what about Sinead?' she queried.

Stephen did not have to think. He knew exactly what his answer would be.

'Sinead's a lovely girl. Much as I care for her, I am not the man for her, nor is she the woman for me. I'll have to break it to her when I get back to Castlehome'.

She deserved honesty from him, not the sort of lies and shabby treatment she had been receiving in recent times.

'It will have to be done very gently because it will probably break her heart.'

Eva was somewhat sorry for what was coming down the tracks for Sinead. However, in love, it is every woman for herself.

Now that he had given Eva an outline of his intentions, a strategy was to be worked out.

Stephen was pushing for a more open approach. While he was tired of sneaking around, he was not sufficiently circumspect to understand Eva's invidious position.

'And what does that mean for us? Meeting in secret is no way to conduct a relationship. Neither is sneaking me into your house when Simon's back is turned. Have you any idea what that is going to do to us long term? While I don't want to push you into anything you wouldn't be happy with. I hope that you can see that our happiness depends on the two of us being together, facing the world together and taking all that it has to throw at us.'

Eva was clearly in a more difficult position than Stephen was. He was a bachelor in temporary employment in a town over a hundred miles from his home. He could do as he pleased. With the possible exception of Sinead, no one was likely to get hurt. However, for her, there was a marriage of fifteen years, as well as two beautiful children to consider. This was notwithstanding her reputation and standing in the community. Only after a great deal of soul searching could she even begin to consider jettisoning all that for the prospect of enduring happiness with a much younger and unproven man.

Yet deep down, her heart was telling her to go for it. She trusted in her feelings for the younger man. No one had ever taken such a hold of her heartstrings as he had.

'I simply don't know where I stand', she began with more than a hint of exasperation in her voice.

'I want you. I desperately want you, and I dread the thought of ever losing you. But I don't know if I dare to accept the consequences of turning my back on my present life,' she lamented.

Stephen attempted to interrupt, but she was insistent on clarifying her position.

'I know that my marriage exists only in name. However, pulling the plug on it is still a very big step to take', she stressed.

'I have to think of what this would do to my girls, how they would react to the scandal of their mother running away with what would be

surely seen as a toyboy. And believe it or not, I would not want to hurt Simon if I did not have to, not to mention my girls'.
Could you imagine it?
Her raised voice underlined the sheer enormity of such a move.

'Simon would have to face the school and entire town, knowing that everyone was talking about him behind his back. It would destroy him. And just imagine my beautiful girls hearing all those nasty things about their mother, running away with her toyboy. It's not a runner Stephen. We have to accept that we cannot be together. We could settle for making the best of moments like this, but that would not be fair on you. You deserve better'.
Stephen did not welcome that remark. On the contrary, he was disappointed and dispirited. Nevertheless, he clung to the hope that his situation might improve.

'As I said, it's up to you. For my part, I know what I have to do. We'll meet when we can, if you have no problem with that. We'll simply take it as it comes.'
Eva stressed that she wished to continue with the relationship despite her better judgment, but it was on terms, which Stephen already considered unsatisfactory. He had little choice but to go along with her preferences.

Thus frustrated by the prospects of his love life, Stephen further referenced the need to sort out his professional life as well.
'I couldn't blame your Simon or any other principal for not extending my contract. I have been a bloody disaster in the classroom for a lot of reasons. For one reason or another, my head has been up my arse. For

the last few weeks, I have let things drift even more. What between drinking at night and lacking focus during the day, my teaching has left much to be desired. It is no exaggeration to say that my classes would have been quieter if I were not in the room at all. That is all because I have been obsessed with you'.

Eva was not sure what to say, so she remained silent.

The secluded nature of the car park allowed them to engage in some restrained form of physical intimacy. Very soon, it was time to drive back to where they had earlier met.

Eva headed to Castlehome while Stephen searched for a card for his parents' silver wedding anniversary. That was coming up on Sunday.

As he sought out the nearest stockist, his mind turned to wonder where he would be in twenty-five years. He wondered whether his love for

Eva would last or not. If today was anything to go by, loving Eva came at a high price.

A shiver ran down his spine when he realised that in twenty-five years, his beloved Eva would be past pension age. He would still be under fifty years of age.

'Jesus Christ, imagine me being married to a woman who was heading for seventy!' he muttered.

His new regime yielded some dividends for Stephen. There had been a temporary but unsustainable improvement in the behaviour of certain classes. The basic problem was that he had already established the unenviable reputation of being a useless teacher who had little control in his classes. It was all so much better for other teachers. It was not so much that the students had been unruly as much as the teacher had been inept.

Paschal O' Meara, a retired teacher, was filling in for Joe Parkes in an adjacent classroom. Joe was a middle-aged man who suffered from respiratory disorders, particularly during the cold and damp days of winter

Sixty-eight years of age, Pascal was delighted to be back in a classroom. He had previously been employed in a neighbouring school as a Guidance Counsellor. Being a very religious man, he was known to take a great interest in young people's moral welfare.

Paschal was also a born actor and a stalwart of the local drama group. Stephen was curious about how the older man would fare with the youngsters.

Whatever the man was doing, it did not sound like Mathematics. There were sounds of furniture being moved, and it certainly wasn't the log tables. The floor was being cleared for some routine or other. Then he heard a succession of shouted commands. An indication of Paschal's self-confidence lay in the fact that he kept his classroom door open. Stephen had a free class. Ordinarily, he would retreat to the staffroom for a coffee. Today, Stephen remained in the adjoining room to listen in on the older man's class.

Paschal spoke in loud, authoritative tones.
'Before you can be fit for any serious study, you must awaken your sleeping bodies. Everyone here, including myself, will do fifteen press-ups. If an old man like me can, then surely you boys can.'
From what Stephen could hear, it sounded like the boys were willing participants in this activity.
Good! Now for some running on the spot.'
The amazing thing was that there were no objections, nor indeed any smart remarks. Paschal was clearly in charge. Stephen was impressed. He recalled that the same crew had made his class a nightmare experience for him. Yet, he was unwilling to fully acknowledge the older man's achievement. He convinced himself that with Paschal, the students were co-conspirators in a flagrant disregard for the curriculum. He rationalised that if Paschal had attempted to talk of theorems or calculus, he might well have floundered too.

After several more minutes of physical workout, the furniture was restored to its proper place. Paschal again called for attention.
'Now, young men, I'm an old man, older than your fathers, maybe older than some of your grandfathers. I've seen the world and lived a full life. You young men, the future leaders of our great country, should learn from my experience. Are there any questions that you would like to ask me?'
Stephen could imagine the students looking at each other for support
'Now, now lads', said Paschal encouragingly.
'Ask me a question on anything at all. Ask about something that may be concerning you'.

Stephen could hear many voices but was unable to identify the boys concerned.

'Were you ever in the army?

'I was in the army until I was thirty-five years of age.'

'Did you ever kill a man?'

'No'

'Do you know how to handle a machine gun?'

'I sure do'.

There was some nervous laughter before the questions went in a predictable direction.

'Do you know how to handle a woman?'

Another chancer amended this question.

'Do you know where to handle them?'

An outburst of lusty laughter ensued. Paschal remained unfazed. It was as if he relished cutting through the predictable juvenilia and then moving onto the really serious business.

'Yes, I know how to handle women', he blurted out confidently.

'The best way is to handle them with respect'.

And yes, I do know where to handle women.'

The inevitable follow-on question came.

'Where?'

'In the state of Matrimony!'

The boys laughed scornfully but had to accept that he was more than a match for them. They posed many pertinent questions about school, career prospects, and matters concerning boy/girl relationships. One lad in the class had some reason to be rather cynical about women. His question queried whether men might be better off without women. Paschal laughed and told the boy that Mark Twain had given the best answer to that particular question.

'What would men be without women? Scarce, Sir, mighty scarce.'

As he listened alone in the silence of his empty room, Stephen saw that Paschal had something very special. The class was spellbound. Normally, he never heard a word through the wall. His class was usually too noisy to hear anything. The biggest shock of all for Stephen was the reaction of the class when the bell rang. There was no stampede for the door, no noisy displacement of furniture, just an appeal to be allowed to stay on there. When this proved impossible, Stephen heard these normally ignorant louts thank Paschal for talking to them. Perhaps the boys learned more in that class period than they would have done had their regular teacher been present. But then, so what? Parkes still had his Maths course to teach. Stephen still had an English course to follow. It is much easier to come in to chat or to entertain.

Paschal handled the class well, but essentially, it was not a class. His was not the role of the tutor, charged with steering the boys through an examination system. If he did the same, it would be a cop-out, and his principal Lynch would tell him so in no uncertain terms.

Stephen was on Study Hall supervision. The principal and three teachers were absent. Simon Lynch was attending a meeting of second-level principals. Mark Mc Gee and Shane Murphy were away with the rugby team while Ellen Hayes had rung in sick.
As Miss Hayes and Shane were free during this class period, Stephen had only Mark Mc Gee's class to supervise. The particular group seemed well behaved. Stephen sat at the back and made a start on marking some exercises. Soon, Stephen's work was interrupted by Jimmy Corrigan's arrival. He pulled in a chair alongside him.
'Hello Stephen, how are things?'
Stephen assured Jimmy that things were just fine.

Corrigan seemed restless, like one who had something to say but was not too sure how to begin. Eventually, he took a deep breath and got to the point with his inimitable tact and diplomacy.
'Daly, are you fucking around with Eva Lynch?'
Stephen had not been expecting this. He was so shocked that he just looked at Corrigan with his mouth hanging open. All the time, his eyes were silently confessing the terrible truth. If he had been caught pissing in the staffroom sink, he couldn't have looked more guilty. There was no point in lying about it. Corrigan would not have spoken if he had not some evidence.
'I've met up with her a few times. How did you find out about it?

'It doesn't matter a damn how I found out. That should be the least of your concern. You should be more worried about who else might find out. Stephen, this is dynamite. Put an end to that relationship as fast as you can. If you let this go on, there will be an awful lot of pain for many people.'

Stephen's natural reaction was to go on the defensive.

'Jimmy, I have done nothing I'm ashamed of.'

Before Stephen could finish his sentence, Corrigan was in again.

'For fucks sake! Don't give me any of that shit. Have you suffered a serious blow to the head, or do you just have a death wish?'

The two men found it difficult to keep their voices down. One or two students turned around to see what was happening. A roar from Jimmy quickly sorted this.

'Turn round, Callaghan, you little runt.'

'It started that night of the First Year Mass. Didn't it? I could sense something was going on'.

'It didn't start till later in the year'.

Jimmy was having none of that.

'That is the night she latched onto you, whether you care to admit it or not'.

Corrigan was determined to open his young colleague's eyes to the seriousness of the matter.

'Think of what would happen if this got out. You could kiss goodbye to any chance of a job here or anywhere else in the country either. Who would employ a teacher who might try to jump the principal's wife?'

Stephen protested that it was nothing as crude as that. He and Eva had something special. He again enquired how Corrigan became aware of it.

'I saw you and her in Dublin when I was visiting my sister's. You were going through the ILAC centre, holding hands like a couple of lovebirds. You were making a damn poor attempt to cover your tracks if you ask me.'

Corrigan predicted that it would all end in tears and urged him to think most carefully before he decided to meet Eva again.

'Talk about shitting on your doorstep! It's even worse. You are shitting on your principal's doorstep. Are there not loads of single women who would be more than willing to oblige you? And where does this leave your lovely Sinead? Are you two-timing her into the bargain?'

The truth can sound very harsh, especially when one is inclined to rationalise the whole business in a more favourable light.

'Jimmy, this is more complicated than you might think. We know the risks involved. I will sort the business out and soon'.

Corrigan understood from this remark that Stephen intended to end the relationship with Eva. He seemed relieved that his intervention had been decisive. Jimmy had done what he came to do. He stood up and patted Stephen on the back before walking towards the door.

In a moment, Jimmy was back. Stooping down, he whispered in his ear.

"Tell me one more thing, Daly. Was she good to go?'

Stephen threw his eyes to heaven.

'Get out, Jimmy, while you're still able to walk out.'

Three weeks into January and Stephen had still not finished with Sinead. Sooner or later, he would have to tell her that it was all over between them. The girl deserved to know. He had been out with her on several occasions since Christmas. On these occasions, it was crystal clear to him that the relationship had run its course. The magic had disappeared.

She didn't call round to the house as frequently as she had done before Christmas. Recently she seemed to be working more nights. Whenever they met now, Sinead appeared to be very tired and more than a little preoccupied. Working nights had taken its toll on her. Her usual sparkle was missing.

The house had become very quiet recently. Tom Clarke was playing music practically every night of the week. When he wasn't performing in Taylor's, he entertained the patrons in the new hotel in Valleyforde. The two lads from the bank were either out courting or participating in the Tennis Club's Winter Leagues. On many evenings Stephen found himself alone in the house. He would spend his evenings flicking through the television channels or looking over his textbooks, trying to keep at least a page ahead of the students.

The situation in class was as bad as ever. Stephen had given up any real hope of turning the tide of discipline in his favour. For him, there had to be a new start in a different school. In the long term, he would perhaps be a better teacher because of this baptism of fire. Lynch seemed to have given up on Stephen as well. He seldom bothered to even speak to him, contenting himself with the odd stony glare. Stephen would be allowed to see out his one-year contract and then be shown the door. He feared to think of the sort of reference he might receive from Lynch. A good reference would be essential if he were to have any real prospect of nailing down a long-term position.

Eva Lynch had a long time for soul-searching and came to accept that she had no future with her husband. This soul searching was of the most painful kind. Her heart was pushing her into the arms of Stephen. Eva needed more time to sanction such a radical move. During their last stolen moments together, she even hypothesised about the logistics of going away with him. They needed to move far away from Castlehome, but what of her girls? That was the crucial question. She would never abandon them.

Dublin, with its teeming population, seemed to offer the greatest possibility of employment for Stephen. For herself, the location was of less consequence; she would have some travelling to do no matter where she was based. Eva was putting Stephen under pressure to end his relationship with Sinead.

'I know that I'm a jealous old cow, but I can't bear the thought of you being with her.'

'Well, you can understand what I think of you continuing to shack up with Simple Simon'.

Eva could easily appreciate that.

It was high time for Stephen to bite the bullet with Sinead at the first real opportunity. That proved to be Wednesday night in Taylor's. He had spent the day rehearsing his speech for the occasion. He intended to present it, not as a termination but rather a trial separation. He would suggest that the problem had been his immaturity. She deserved better. It would be a case of:

'It's not you; it's me.'

Fortified with these arguments and a measure of brandy, he sat down alongside Sinead in a dimly lit recess of the pub.

Sinead looked ill at ease as she sipped anxiously from a glass of lager. Stephen was having difficulty in forcing the moment to a crisis. After some rather stilted conversation concerning the chilly conditions outside, he was staggered to hear Sinead apologise in advance for what she was about to say. He sat back to listen, dreading that perhaps she would suggest getting engaged for Valentine's Day.

However, when she began to speak, he was rendered speechless. Sinead, the intended victim, was giving him the elbow.

'Stephen, you're a nice man and all that, but this relationship is going nowhere. I do not think that we are meant for each other. It's as simple as that.'

She looked to him for some reaction. It was not forthcoming, so she continued. It was clear that he was not the only one who had rehearsed a breakup speech.

'I felt that there was always something missing, some.... vital ingredient. It is only recently that I have realised what that is'.

Stephen was too shocked even to ask the obvious question. He continued to stare blankly at her. She continued with what had almost become a monologue.

'Chemistry, that is what is missing. You see, you are decent and kind. We can have a really good time together. The problem is that you don't excite me. Do you understand what I mean?'

The irony was the situation was not lost on Stephen. Sinead had not spent the day fine-tuning her words, making them as mild and inoffensive as possible and then she tosses this grenade into the mix.

'Excite her, the deceptive bitch', Stephen thought silently.

'If I had put my mind to it, I could have had her as high as a kite on chemistry'.

When he did not answer, she repeated the question, unwittingly twisting the knife, which she had so coldly plunged into his heart.

'Do you understand what I'm saying?'

Stephen had been hurt. The baser side of him wished to retaliate for this perceived onslaught on his manhood. There was no point in exacerbating an already difficult situation.

'Yea, I know what you're saying. You are giving me the heave-ho, and you are in the market for a man with a bit more chemistry'.

That was about the height of it.

'If you haven't already found him! Have you another bloke lined up?'

She did not respond, hoping that he would not continue to press her on that point. She had said what she had come to say.

It was now time to go. She declined his offer of a lift home and was glad to walk out the doors of the bar, a free woman again.

As she exited, she turned back in time to catch Stephen raise his pint glass to the barman to signal a refill. He would deal with disappointment in his own way.

Stephen nursed his second pint for some time, mulling over the events of the evening. Even though the evening had produced the desired result anyway, Sinead had delivered a devastating blow to his ego. He was still registering shock as he sat alone, stunned at how she had so cruelly turned the tables on him.

Reaching for his mobile phone, he dialled Eva's number. He had promised to let her know how events unfolded. She was staying overnight in a hotel in Ennis.

As Eva answered, Stephen injected a false note of triumph into his tone 'Mission accomplished! Everything went according to plan'.

Eva sounded relieved. She asked how Sinead had received the news.

'There were a few tears and lots of questioning, but she'll be alright in time. I'm sure she'll meet up with someone new soon.'

Tom Clarke sat alone in the house, vacantly watching a video he had hired for the night. He knew that by now, Sinead would have broken the news to Stephen. He wondered how his colleague and housemate would take it while hoping that it would not give rise to an ugly scene between them. Sinead had promised him that she would keep his name completely out of it and would, if pushed, deny that there was anyone else on the scene.

He and Sinead would continue to meet secretly away from prying eyes; then, after a decent interval, they would go public. There would be the annual *Nurses' Ball* in early March. The plan was to invite her friend Tom to be her escort, which would develop into a courtship. That would raise no eyebrows. Even Stephen would have no reason to feel aggrieved.

Tom had always fancied Sinead. He would have asked her out months ago, but Stephen beat him to it. Sinead's position began to change after she had been in Dublin with Stephen. She suspected that Stephen was deliberately keeping her at arm's length. More serious doubts flooded into her mind. She spoke about these concerns to Tom. The more they talked, the more Sinead realised that she had no future with Stephen Daly.

Over the Christmas period, when everybody else was out of town, Tom and Sinead had kept each other company. It was during this period that their relationship blossomed. Her story about spending an extra few days with her family was simply a means to an end. She wanted to spend precious time with her newfound love. With two empty houses on the estate during that week, they could have all the time in the world to be together.

Sinead could never have imagined the real reason behind Stephen's ongoing disregard for her. Not surprisingly, she began to doubt her attractiveness to members of the opposite sex. Being with Tom provided her with much-needed reassurance on that front. He lavished his full attention on her and made her feel special in a way that Stephen felt unable to do.

It was just after midnight when Stephen stumbled into the living room, looking a bit the worse for wear. He had wisely left his car at the pub and walked home.

Tom turned down the volume on the TV and tried to act as normally as possible. He did not like being duplicitous with his housemate. He liked even less the prospect of a blazing row with him.

'Hello there, I didn't hear your car'.

'No, I had a few too many to drink. It was safer to walk home. You might give me a lift as far as the pub before school to collect my car'.

'Not a bother!'

'Tom, I have a bit of news for you. Sinead and I have split up.'

Tom did a good job of feigning surprise.

'Wow! I had not seen that coming.'

'I know what you mean. We had been in a rut for a while, and it was high time to do something about it.'

Tom was relieved that Stephen had not figured out the true situation. Sinead must have handled the situation very well.

'Come on, sit down here, I'll make you a cup of strong coffee.'
'Thanks, Tom, but it's Sinead I'm concerned for. She didn't take it too well. I hope she doesn't do anything foolish'.
Tom could not believe what he was hearing. Stephen had been unceremoniously ditched, yet he was pretending that he was the one who ended the relationship. He couldn't wait to tell this to Sinead. She would be shocked by his deception.
Tom decided to probe some more.
'So, Sinead wanted to continue seeing you. Did she?'
'Yea, she did, but I had to be firm. You have to be cruel to be kind. Incidentally, if you are talking to Sinead, don't say that I told you what happened. I said that I would let her say that it was her idea to finish it'.
'Ah, you were always a true gentleman, Stephen'.
Tom went to the kitchen to boil up the kettle, smiling his self-satisfied smile. The business had turned out as well as it could.

Having lain low and licked his wounds for some days, Stephen Daly was ready to face the world again. With Sinead off the scene, he was a free man again. The only regret that he had about the entire business was that he didn't chuck her before she had jilted him.

He was now free to give Eva his undivided attention. Recently, they had taken to meeting up well away from Castlehome. Depending on Eva's movements, they would meet on the Dublin or Galway roads on any given day. It was far from being an ideal arrangement. Meeting Eva at her home was slightly more problematic of late. Old Simon was becoming less predictable in his movements. On the previous Friday evening, Simon Lynch nearly happened upon them.

Eva had called Stephen earlier to say that her husband was due at a school meeting at eight-thirty. Stephen parked his car in the grounds of the Castlehome Arms and continued from there on foot to Eva's house.

Eva herself was also very vigilant in these matters. She would leave a side window open under the curtains to stand a better chance of hearing Simon's car return. She was also particularly careful recently not to leave any signs of a visitation when her husband returned. There were no extra cups in the dishwasher, no smudged makeup on her face and no lingering smells of aftershave. She took to burning fragrant oils each evening, so whenever Stephen called, there would be no tell-tale fragrances. Short of having surveillance cameras in the house, there was nothing to indicate that she ever had a visitor.

On the day in question, Stephen had reached her back door when he heard a car on the driveway. He had to hide. He noticed some

shrubbery at the gable of the house and he ran to seek cover there.
There was a real danger of being discovered.
He lay still and waited to see how the situation unfolded.
In a matter of minutes, the car started again. He thought it advisable to wait for some further moments before reappearing. Finally, he ventured out from the shrubbery and approached the window to give his coded knock.
Eva had still her hand on her heart. She was only beginning to recover her breath after the narrow escape. Even she wasn't aware of precisely how close they had come to being detected.
Stephen wondered about Lynch's checking of all the rooms.
'Do you think he's on to us?'
'I don't think so. Simon had documents and files all over the house. He couldn't remember where he left the particular ones he was looking for'.
'Does he treat the house as a sort of office?'
'He sure does. You couldn't move without tripping over school-related papers. It's an awful curse'.
Stephen could not understand how Lynch could have so many reminders of his work in his home.

'That would drive me crazy. I try not to bring home any copybooks if I can manage it. They are only reminders of work, and I can't relax while I can see the bloody things'.
Eva considered that they could both do with a strong drink.
'The sound of the car approaching put the heart crossways in me. I need a good strong drink'.

She proceeded to pour herself a large brandy.

'My heart is still pounding from the shock'.

Despite knowing that Simon was most unlikely to return, Eva and Stephen were not the better of that for the rest of the evening. They could not relax and had one ear constantly alert for any engine noise changes near the house.

After spending some time with Eva, Stephen decided to go home early. There was no point in asking for trouble.

On Valentine's night, Stephen held Eva in his arms. They exchanged love tokens while classic love songs played in the background. The night was cold and frosty, but that was not a problem. It was warm where they were, up in the front seats with a perfect view of the starry heavens. They were not in a fancy restaurant or a trendy city nightclub but sitting in the front seats of Stephen Daly's parked car in a lay by, just outside of Longford town. The only music came from a cassette tape in the stereo. The car engine was running to maintain a warm atmosphere. Despite the circumstances, both were extremely happy.

Eva had finally decided on her future. The relief was priceless. She was going to leave her husband and join Stephen as soon as he finished in Castlehome. Between now and then, he would seek employment for next September in the Greater Dublin area. He would call on a few well-placed connections for their support in this regard. For the summer months, he would get a job on the buildings with his Uncle Pat, a major sub-contractor in the city.

Eva would not tell her daughters until the summer holidays were upon them. It was better not to offer any distractions during the school year. Eva felt confident that the girls would come around to accept the idea when they got over the initial shock. Naturally, they could see their father any time they would wish to do so, which she guessed would not be very often. There was the matter of accommodation in the city. However, there was no great rush with that. They still had three months to sort that problem out.

Stephen knew that his family would not look too kindly on his relationship with Eva. He knew that they would see it as not only sinful but as throwing his life away. There was no chance at all of his getting their blessing. The best he could hope for would be that in time they might talk to him again. Never would they accept Eva or her daughters. Both his father and mother had met Sinead and were fond of her.

His mother constantly suggested that perhaps Sinead might be the one for him. Stephen had not even bothered to tell his parents that he and Sinead had gone their separate ways. He did not see any point in doing so. Despite his parents' predictable objections, Stephen felt that Eva was the only woman for him. He could be happy with her, something that he might never be with anyone else.

All good things must come to an end. At ten o'clock, it was time for Eva to transfer to her car. It was their pattern for Eva to get a five-minute head start on Stephen for the return journey to Castlehome. That way, they would not arouse suspicions by travelling together or arriving simultaneously, even in separate cars.

Eva was sitting, half in and half out of the passenger seat of Stephen's car. She had one foot on the road, ready for off. Just then, she spotted the colourful paper wallet, a sure indication of recently developed photographs. Stephen had collected them earlier in the day.

'Anything interesting here?'

'No, just the usual family snaps'.

'Are you in any of them?'

'Unfortunately, yes.'

Eva opened the packet and casually thumbed through them, making the odd polite enquiry as to the subjects.

'They are not great. I was the official photographer on the night. That alone will tell you something about the level of expertise involved. Remember I told you about my parents' twenty-fifth wedding anniversary party. The film was sitting in the camera for weeks. I took it out yesterday and had them developed.'

Eva scrutinised the snaps, holding some photos directly under the courtesy light to get a better view.

'Who are these people? Are they relations of yours, Stephen?'

'Like I said, those are my parents'.

Who else were they likely to be?

Eva seemed fixated on that particular photograph.

'Well, am I like either of them?'

She seemed strangely mystified concerning the whole thing.

'You told me that your parents were from Dublin '.

Stephen could not figure out what that had to do with anything.

Eva's face registered a mixture of confusion and horror.

'I don't understand'.

'You don't understand what?

He questioned her again, but she seemed to be struggling to understand something, which seemed to puzzle her.

She had a question for Stephen.

'Did you always live in Dublin?' she asked.

'I have lived there since I started school. When I was a kid, we lived in Portlaoise. There's a long and sad story and tonight is certainly not the night to share it. Anyway, most Dublin people originate down the country'.

Her cold hands lost their grip on the photographs. These tumbled into the well of the car.
Stephen stooped to pick them up and replaced them in the paper wallet. The cold air entering the car was already freezing up the windows. Eva looked as if she was going to pass out with the cold. The blood seemed to have drained from Eva's face. Even her lips had lost their colour. It was no night to be sitting with the car door open.
'Come on, Eva, close the door or get back to your car if you're going now. I'm frozen solid here".
Eva stepped out of the car. Stephen held her close.
'God, you are cold. You're trembling like a leaf. You'd better get indoors quickly. Better say goodnight so'.
Kissing her softly on the cheek, he whispered that he loved her.

One week later, the bombshell was dropped. No one in the school could believe it. It defied belief. Nobody could have imagined what was going on under their noses. Both of the individuals involved had seemed so proper and respectable. It was a classic case of still waters running deep.

When Stephen arrived for his quarter to ten class, the teachers were all in the staff room, still trying to process the news.

Stephen asked Tom, who was scratching his head in amazement.

'What on earth has happened?'

'You'll never believe it', he replied, trying to suppress a laugh.

'It seems that Simon Lynch has run away with Ellen Hayes. Can you fucking credit it?'

Stephen was as shocked as the rest of them. He had not seen this coming. This sensational news carried an extra significance for him. He asked Tom how this news had broken.

'Both of them were away for the last couple of days, supposedly at meetings. It appears that Father Sweeney got some sort of note from the two of them this morning. It appears that they have run off together. The priest is coming over at break time to tell us about it. Isn't it some laugh?'

It was certainly mind-boggling stuff, but he did not see it as a laughing matter.

Tom could not credit it at all.

'Ellen Hayes, for Christ's sake! Does the man have any taste at all? Sure, he had a lot better than that at home, the stupid fucker'.

Nobody noticed when Stephen Daly left the building and walked to his car. He needed to call Eva and get her view on the development. It must have come as a terrible surprise to her.

She wasn't answering her mobile, so he tried her landline. When she answered, her tone of voice indicated that she was in a state of shock or even distress. It had been as big a bombshell for her as for all of the others.

Stephen offered to call over to the house, but that was not possible. Eva had been inundated with callers. Scandalous news certainly travels fast.

Over the telephone, Eva admitted to Stephen that the news had flattened her. He broke it to her by letter. It was not a scribbled note left on the table or the like. He had posted the letter to her. It had arrived in the post that morning.

'He wrote to tell me that he had gone to London with this Ellen Hayes woman. He said that he would be in touch later to 'formalise our separation'. There was also something, which had particular relevance for Stephen.

'Simon may have also have known about us. He said that I would have no difficulty getting a younger man to keep me happy'.

Stephen was not unduly concerned.

He presumed that it was just a reference to Eva's good looks. Time would soon tell.

At the eleven o'clock break, the Superior of the order addressed the assembled staff. He seemed ill at ease and uncomfortable in the role. He confirmed that Simon Lynch and Ellen Hayes had both submitted their resignations, with immediate effect. They were already out of the jurisdiction. Both had recorded separate apologies for any embarrassment or inconvenience caused by their actions. Rev. Sweeney moved to confirm Mr Raymond Shaw as Acting Principal. Mr Sean O'Reilly, the senior History teacher, would serve as Acting Vice-principal. They would hire a substitute teacher to take charge of Miss Hayes's classes.

The cleric termed the whole business 'regrettable' and urged the staff to support the new management team.

Unsurprisingly, there was no other conversation topic among staff or pupils for the rest of the day. Now, with the benefit of hindsight, many recalled a particular closeness between the two fugitives. Some of the more imaginative students claimed to have seen the two fugitives in a state of undress in the old library. Most people rightly treated such reports with scepticism, but some would not dismiss them. They were living in strange times.

Everyone in the town had heard of the developments. Nobody could quite believe that two such stalwarts of Catholic conservatism should be the ones involved in such a lurid affair.

On the other hand, many felt sympathy for Eva and her two girls. Simon emerged from the affair with considerable reputational damage, but he still had his defenders.

Ellen Hayes was not very well known in town. She had been such a retiring personality that very few knew anything about her. However, students, whom she had taught, reflected on her decency and professionalism. There was little doubt but that Ellen Hayes had been a model professional up until she fell victim to the charms of her principal. Despite this, some continued to paint Ellen Hayes in the unlikely roles of scarlet lady and home wrecker.

Little did anyone know that the Lynch marriage was already in peril. Eva, whom nobody had suspected of duplicity, had been considering making her exit from that marital setup.

Stephen Daly had been frustrated in his efforts to have a conversation with her. There always seemed to be someone with her, supporting her in this time of crisis.

When he eventually managed to get Eva alone, she was still troubled. He tried his best to make her see the positive side of the shock departures. He explained that she would be seen as a victim rather than as the scarlet woman who walked out on her respectable husband into the arms of a younger man.

He argued she could leave the area in summer. No tongues would wag at all. The word might never filter through to Castlehome that she and he were together. Anyway, there would certainly be no grounds for presuming that there had been a relationship in place before her husband's departure.

Eva was in no mood to be reassured on anything relating to her husband's disappearance. The harsh reality of a marriage breakup had registered with her. In a very real sense, she was mourning a death rather than celebrating a departure.

Stephen had not factored into his calculations any ambivalence on Eva's part. He had foolishly presumed that she could put all those years of marriage behind her and blithely run away with him. Stephen could see similarities between this breakup and his parting with Sinead. He resented the fact that both he and Eva had been beaten to the draw when it came to giving the elbow to a partner. Life can throw up some very cruel twists of fate.

Eva had more pressing matters on her mind. She not yet told the girls about their father's departure with Ellen Hayes.

Having left Eva, Stephen dropped in for a nightcap to Taylors. There was but one topic of conversation there. The pub seemed to have benefited from the scandal. Many people, who might otherwise have remained at home, had come out to hear the latest instalment. But, as is often the case, the story had been embellished with each telling. In some versions, Simon Lynch took the college heating money with him. More doubtful accounts had the ageing Ellen Hayes pregnant with twins. Jimmy Corrigan, who had been standing at the bar, noticed Stephen's arrival. He made his way over to him. Pulling him by the sleeve, he whispered in his ear.

'Are you not glad that you dropped Eva Lynch when you did? Otherwise, you would be saddled with her and those two kids for the rest of your life. That would knock the romance out of you'.

Stephen nodded his head.

‘I suppose you are right, Jimmy. But today's events are so very strange, aren't they?'
Jimmy was philosophical.
'When it comes to affairs of the heart, you can never tell what the upshot will be. Still, I have to admit that I never thought Simon Lynch had it in him, the randy old goat. Jaysus, can you imagine them at it. The very thought would put you off your drink', he mused.
'But what will he do for money over in England, Jimmy?’
'Money won't be a worry for him. He has enough service to be entitled to a decent lump sum and pension. He will not need to work over there, and I'm sure his scarlet woman will get a job handy enough'.

Tom Clarke had been booked to play music in the pub that night, but Shay Taylor rightly presumed that no one would want to listen to music. They might even consider music might impede the free flow of information and gossip on the affair.
The newly redundant Tom sipped his beer and joined in the speculation and conjecture. Then, when he saw Stephen, he made his way towards him in what seemed a most casual approach but was, in fact, a clever and rehearsed move.

'By the way, Sinead O'Shea has invited me to the Nurses' Ball next month. I did not give her an answer yet because I wanted to clear it with you. Maybe you two have some sort of understanding yet'.

Stephen reached out his hand and lightly punched Tom on the shoulder. 'Tom, Sinead and I are history. You go for it, and the best of luck to you. Be careful with her, though. She can be a hard woman to figure out'.

The surreal atmosphere in St. Jude's lingered for days. The Acting Principal, Raymond Shaw, manfully attempted to maintain some semblance of normality, but it had been an uphill struggle. Reporters from some of the tabloid publications had descended on the area to glean additional sordid details on the affair for their salacious stories. There was strict observance of the 'No Comment' line from the school authorities. That did not deter the intrepid reporters. They spent the day in the pubs, shops and restaurants, piecing together a profile on the two runaways. It was made clear that they would pay good money for the right sort of information.

The previous night had seen a particularly heavy fall of snow. The temperature never succeeded in getting above freezing point during the day, while the town's streets were dangerously slippery underfoot. Owing to the dangerous conditions, and the prospect of further heavy snow showers, Raymond Shaw decided to close the school at three o'clock and keep it closed until Monday morning. Despite the chill, Castlehome was nevertheless a hotbed of rumour and speculation.

Due to the freezing conditions, postal deliveries were also behind schedule. Arriving home at three o'clock, Stephen met the postman at the gate. Lying on the mat, inside the door, was a letter for him. The name and address on the envelope had been typed. He presumed it to be the usual promotional material from a financial institution. The letter could wait. It was left unopened on the kitchen table until nine o'clock that night. When he finally opened it, he discovered that it was far from being a circular from a lending agency.

Stephen's eyes skipped down to the signature at the bottom of the handwritten page. His heart skipped a beat as he saw the familiar initials of his former principal. He wondered why on earth Simon Lynch would be writing to him. With bated breath, he began to read from the top of the letter.

Daly,

You probably think that you have been very clever, sneaking around behind my back. The truth is that you have been anything but clever. You are as deficient in your private life as you are in the classroom. Don't flatter yourself that you can ever make Eva happy. Right now, you are smitten with Eva. That is understandable in someone so immature. I should warn you that you are out of your depth. Eva would gobble you up before breakfast and still have an appetite for something substantial. I can guarantee you that you won't be as keen on her when you discover the truth.

Ask about Portlaoise. If she does not tell you the truth, then I will take pleasure in doing so. Here's hoping that you have the strength of character to make something of your life when you are finished with Eva and with Castlehome.

SL

PS

Remind Eva that she will be hearing from my solicitor. That is if you are still talking to her.

Stephen was rooted to the spot. He stood there, letter in hand until his muscles momentarily relaxed. This was followed by some moments of involuntary shaking. The reference to Portlaoise raised alarm bells in his head. He vividly recalled their conversation on Valentine's night. Eva had displayed an undue interest in the photograph. But what was the connection?

There are some things one never forgets. Stephen clearly recalled that the young woman's name had been Ann Mc Ateer. She had been alone in her car on that fateful day, so what on earth was the connection with Eva?

A dazed Stephen Daly drove recklessly through the town's deserted streets and up the ice-covered hill to Eva Lynch's home. The slipping and sliding of the tyres on the glassy roads mirrored the disjointed nature of his thoughts as he desperately sought to make sense of Lynch's letter. It was clear from the obnoxious tone of Lynch's correspondence that Eva had highly sensitive information. The imminent disclosure of that information would most likely bring him renewed anguish.

On this occasion, Stephen drove into her driveway, oblivious to any considerations of propriety. A sense of urgency had overwhelmed him, and good manners had become the first casualty of his single-minded focus on the mystery of Portlaoise. His finger stubbornly sat on the doorbell until she answered the door.

Eva, who was already distressed at the recent turn of events, was further perturbed by a premonition of impending calamity. The unseemly ringing of the bell could only be attributed to an agitated Stephen. That meant the imminent encounter was likely to be horrendously emotional.

When she opened the door to him, the young man's distraught expression confirmed her suspicions.

Stephen roughly thrust Simon's letter into her face. With an accusing look in his wild eyes, he pushed past her into the front room. Her explanation needed to be good.

Eva sobbed as she held the letter in her trembling hands, solemnly scanning the few lines of the ill-boding note. A sudden bout of dizziness and nausea seized her. Reaching out for some form of

support, she grabbed the back of a nearby chair. The chair failed to support her faltering weight.
Collapsing in a pitiful heap on the floor, she held her shaking head in both hands.
A near deranged Stephen was insensible to her plight. His mind focussed only on the words that might flow from her quivering lips.
'Come on. Spit it out! I am waiting.' he angrily demanded.
Eva snatched a paper tissue from her sleeve, attempted to clear her airways for speech.
'As God is my judge, I swear that I never saw the car until it was too late.'
That terrible admission had removed any lingering hope that they could start a new life together. The passage of time had done nothing to lessen her pain or regret. She could barely speak, but Stephen deserved an explanation, and she was determined to give him one.
'I was changing channels on the car radio. I could not have looked down for more than a split second.'
Stephen struggled to absorb all of what he was hearing.
'How the hell could it have been you? Your name is not Mc Ateer. Ann was her name, not Eva.'
He was merely clutching at straws, desperately hoping that what he knew in his heart to be true might not be so. He wanted Eva to tell him anything, which would distance her from his childhood tragedy. She was unable to do so. There was nothing left to cling onto. The tears began to flow down his cheeks as she revived the terrible memory. He was growing increasingly unstable with each passing moment.

'Oh, Jaysus!' Eva remained on the floor, curled into a ball as she cried like a baby. Stephen could not feel it in his heart to sympathise with her plight.

'I was a child at the time, but I've lived for seventeen years with that blasted Mc Ateer name.'

There was no response from Eva.

She could not find the words to articulate her feelings.

'Mc Ateer is your maiden name. Isn't it?' he said, lowering himself into a sitting position, with his back to the wall.

'Then why did they call you Ann?'

She wanted to answer his questions. At the very least, he was entitled to that.

'My first name was Ann. Therefore, it was the name on my charge sheet', she answered.

'And the papers used that name too', she sobbed.

'Oh, it's so bloody awful. I was just a silly young teenager driving up to some useless seminar in Dublin. I'll never forget that moment or the aftermath. I nearly cracked up completely. I had to spend three weeks in a psychiatric institution'.

'Why, why, why did it have to be you? Only for you, Conor would still be alive today. What did you want with the fucking radio in the first place? You must have seen the car. You couldn't have been that blind or stupid.'

As she again recalled the tragic moments, she attempted to stem the river of tears, which flowed down her cheeks

'The court was a nightmare for everyone involved. I will never forget the accusing look on your parents' faces as they looked at me across the courtroom. Naturally, they look older now, but I instantly recognised them in that damned photograph. I can still see the pain in their eyes and their accusing looks. It was a living nightmare.'

Her words now came more freely as she no longer had to compose her thoughts. Instead, she was now giving voice to sentiments, which she had often rehearsed in her troubled mind in the intervening years.

'I often imagine that it had been a nightmare and wish that one day I will wake up from it. Not until that night did I ever dream that you could be anything but a namesake of those unfortunate people.'

Eva's cries were increasing in intensity. She was now shrieking.

'I killed your twin brother', she said, fists clenched and shaking.

'But I didn't mean to. I killed your baby brother, but I didn't mean to'.

Stephen was not listening to her. He just lay crouched in the corner of the room, repeatedly striking his fists off the wall. He was striking the wall with such ferocity that his knuckles were bleeding profusely. This blood flowed in little streaks down the wallpaper and right onto the white skirting board.

'You must realise that it was an accident. It was just a terrible, tragic accident that has haunted me for every day of the past seventeen years. I had tried to banish it from my head, but I could never succeed in doing that.'

The only other person who knew was her husband, Simon. She only came clean with him after she had seen the photograph of Stephen's parents. Her story to Simon was that the young teacher had been showing them to his girlfriend in the Chinese takeaway when she caught a glimpse of it as she waited for her order to be served.

Eva, still clutching her husband's note, had recalled the nightmare of that terrible day for Stephen, but she could see that he was not listening. He had not heard a single word of it. His ears had been closed, but his heart was full of anger and bitterness.

After some moments of whimpering and lamentation, Stephen rose from his crouched position. A violent compulsion had taken hold of him. He lashed out at every piece of furniture in his path. He tossed a crystal decanter into the fireplace. Angrily grabbing the coffeepot, he slammed it through the glass-topped table.

With his anger somewhat dissipated, Stephen turned more silent and still. Eva looked on with alarm and horror as she observed a distressing transformation taking place in the young man who had won her heart. Even though he was looking in her direction, his eyes were looking past her.

All of a sudden, he ran to the door shouting excitedly. He was no longer the man but was a child again. He was about to leave on an exciting outing with his family.

'Wait for me, Conor! We'll race to the car.

The winner gets to sit in the front seat'.

In his demented state, Stephen ran out into the snow-covered driveway, regressing to the time when he was back with his little brother, running to see which of them would be first to their father's car.

Eva rose to her feet and ran to the open door, woefully anticipating the worst-case scenario. She heard the engine roar into life and saw the headlights light up the driveway. Her tear-filled eyes followed the car's progress as it sped furiously down the hill in the direction of the town. The moment it slipped out of sight, Eva dropped to her knees and made the sign of the cross.

'God protect him', she implored.

The bar of the Castlehome Arms fell silent at the sickening sound of the impact. Customers and staff ran outside to investigate. Some were compelled to avert their eyes.

The sight of the trapped body in the mangled and smoking wreckage gave rise to a moment's paralysis. Then a few of those present made the sign of the cross.

The Emergency Services arrived and took control of the situation. An eerie silence descended on the town as people struggled to come to terms with this latest turn of events.

At two minutes to midnight, the local garda sergeant called to a Dublin presbytery. He requested the priest's assistance in breaking some tragic news to one of his parishioners. As the two men drove to the particular address, the sergeant briefed the priest on the sad details.

'They say that God moves in mysterious ways, Father, but the likes of this defies any explanation'.

'I often think, Sergeant, that God will have an awful lot of explaining to do if we ever meet up with Him'

'And according to what I hear, Father, the lad's twin brother also died in a road accident some years ago'.

The priest shook his head in shock.

'O my God! A twin tragedy!'

The ashen-faced sergeant took a deep breath before he rang the doorbell.

'This is a part of the job I hate most'.

'You and me, both', replied the priest.

Both men could hear the bell ringing inside the house.

They instinctively knew that this bell would change that family's life forever more.

The two men lifted their heads as a light suddenly appeared in an upstairs window. Frank Daly opened the bedroom window and scrutinised on the solemn pair in their respective uniforms.

Without a word being uttered, he knew that his world was about to be delivered another paralysing blow.

It was the priest who spoke.

'We are so sorry to disturb you, Frank, but, I'm afraid we have some bad news for you'.

Frank Daly nodded his understanding.

'I'm on my way down', he responded.

Printed in Great Britain
by Amazon